What You Can Do About ADHD

CONTEMPORARY DISEASES AND DISORDERS

What You Can Do About ADHD

Monique Vescia, Alvin and Virginia Silverstein, and Laura Silverstein Nunn

Enslow Publishing
101 W. 23rd Street
Suite 240
New York, NY 10011
USA

enslow.com

Published in 2016 by Enslow Publishing, LLC
101 W. 23rd Street, Suite 240, New York, NY 10011

Copyright © 2016 by Alvin and Virginia Silverstein, and Laura Silverstein Nunn

Enslow Publishing materials © 2016 by Enslow Publishing, LLC

All rights reserved.

No part of this book may be reproduced by any means without the written permission of the publisher.

Cataloging-in-Publication Data
Vescia, Monique.
  What you can do about ADHD / by Monique Vescia, Alvin and Virginia Silverstein, and Laura Silverstein Nunn.
     p. cm. — (Contemporary diseases and disorders)
  Includes bibliographical references and index.
  ISBN 978-0-7660-7028-8 (library binding)
   1. Attention-deficit hyperactivity disorder — Juvenile literature. 2. Hyperactive children — Juvenile literature. I. Vescia, Monique. II. Title.
  RJ506.H9 V47 2016
  618.92'8589—d23

Printed in the United States of America

To Our Readers: We have done our best to make sure all Web site addresses in this book were active and appropriate when we went to press. However, the author and the publisher have no control over and assume no liability for the material available on those Web sites or on any Web sites they may link to. Any comments or suggestions can be sent by e-mail to customerservice@enslow.com.

Portions of this book originally appeared in the book *The ADHD Update: Understanding Attention-Deficit/Hyperactivity Disorder.*

Disclaimer: For many of the images in this book, the people photographed are models. The depictions do not imply actual situations or events.

Photo Credits: Alexilus/Shutterstock.com, p. 45; Antonio Guillem/Shutterstock.com, p. 75; © AP Images, pp. 9, 63, 93; © Bob Daemmrich / Alamy, p. 32; Brendan Smialowski/Getty Images News/Getty Images, p. 92; Caitlin Teal Price/For the Washington Post via Getty Images, pp. 39, 61, 77; Carol & Mike Werner/Visuals Unlimited, Inc./Visuals Unlimited/Getty Images, p. 3; Chris Coduto/Getty Images Sport/Getty Images, p. 91; Creatas Images/Thinkstock, p. 53; DEA/G. DAGLIORTI/Getty Images, p. 15; Dominique Charriau/ Getty Images Europe/Getty Images, p. 34; Hulton Archive/Getty Images, p. 19; Jb Reed/Bloomberg via Getty Images, p. 54; JGI/Tom Grill/Blend Images/Getty Images, p. 73; Joe Raedle/ Getty Images North America/Getty Images, pp. 24, 89; Juli Leonard/Raleigh News & Observer/MCT via Getty Images, p. 71; Karl Gehring/The Denver Post via Getty Images, p. 70; l i g h t p o e t/ Shutterstock.com, p. 11; Lorraine Swanson/Shutterstock.com, p. 79; luchschen/iStock/Thinkstock, p. 12; Michael Du Cille/The Washington Post/Getty Images, p. 67; PARK JI_HWAN/AFP/Getty Images, pp. 84, 86; Paul Burns/Blend Images/Thinkstock, p. 58; PHILIPPE MERLE?AFP Getty Images, p. 83; Steve Liss/The LIFE Images Collection/Getty Images, p. 41; stockernumber2/Shutterstock.com, p. 47; Susan Watts/ NY Daily News via Getty Images, p. 69; Three Lions/Hulton Archive/Getty Images, p. 22; ullstein bild/Getty images, p. 16; Urbano Delvalle/The LIFE Images Collection/Getty Images, p. 30; wavebreakmedia/Shutterstock.com, p. 36.

Cover Credits: Carol & Mike Werner/Visuals Unlimited, Inc./Visuals Unlimited/Getty Images (ADHD concept art).

Contents

	ADHD at a Glance	6
1	Life in Overdrive	8
2	ADHD Throughout History	14
3	Understanding ADHD	29
4	Diagnosing and Treating ADHD	51
5	Living Well With ADHD	72
6	Future Directions in Research and Treatment	81
	Top 10 Questions and Answers	95
	Timeline of ADHD	97
	Chapter Notes	100
	Glossary	105
	For More Information	108
	Further Reading	110
	Index	111

ADHD at a Glance

WHAT IS IT?

ADHD is a common behavioral condition that causes problems in three main areas: inability to focus or pay attention (inattention), being overly active (hyperactivity), and acting without thinking first (impulsivity).

WHO GETS IT?

It is most often identified in school-age children, but many of them will continue to have the condition as adults. ADHD is diagnosed three times more often in boys than in girls. This is not because girls are less prone to the disorder; the ADHD symptoms girls exhibit are often more subtle and less stereotypical than those of boys.

HOW DO YOU GET IT?

The cause of ADHD is not known. There is strong evidence that the condition is inherited, passed from generation to generation. Many experts also believe that environmental factors play a role in the development of ADHD. These factors include brain injury; exposure to tobacco, alcohol, and other drugs in the womb; and harmful chemicals in the environment.

WHAT ARE THE SYMPTOMS?

Not being able to pay attention is a main symptom. Hyperactivity is also commonly seen, especially in young children. Impulsive behavior and being easily distracted are also common.

HOW ARE THE SYMPTOMS TREATED?

A combination of some or all of the following are usually used: behavior therapy, school counseling, social skills training, and medication. Exercise may also help people with ADHD to regain focus. Schools are usually involved in the treatment of ADHD students.

HOW CAN IT BE PREVENTED?

Since the cause of ADHD is unknown, no one knows yet whether or not it can be prevented. Successful treatment of people with ADHD may help lessen their symptoms so that they can be more focused and less impulsive.

Chapter 1

LIFE IN OVERDRIVE

Imagine trying to swing a bat at just the right instant to connect with a baseball coming at you at 90 miles per hour (145 kph). Then picture trying to hit that blazing fastball at just the right spot when your attention keeps wandering. When Andrés "Yungo" Torres signed on with the Detroit Tigers at age twenty, he dreamed of playing ball in the major leagues. Instead, he spent fourteen frustrating years struggling in the minors. He didn't know what was wrong, but his batting average was low, he missed signals, and he had trouble seeing the pitch properly when he was at bat.

In 2002 Torres was diagnosed with attention-deficit/hyperactivity disorder, or ADHD, but he ignored his diagnosis and refused treatment—a decision that almost cost him his career. Gene Roof, a coach for the Tigers whose son has ADHD, urged Torres to seek treatment. Finally, in 2009 Torres agreed to try medication, and his performance dramatically improved. Just a year later, Torres had made it to the majors, and signed on with the San Francisco Giants. As the starting center fielder, Torres helped the Giants defeat the Texas Rangers in the 2010 World

Series, the team's first series win since 1954. That same year Torres won the Willie Mac award, named after Hall of Famer Willie McCovey, for spirit and leadership.

Torres's journey is the subject of a documentary film called *Gigante* ("giant" in Spanish). The film's director and producer also had struggled with ADHD, and they were drawn to the story of the ballplayer who accepts his diagnosis and is finally able to realize his major league dreams. They hoped Torres's story would inspire other young people living with the disorder. The film makes it clear that even with medication, acute ADHD is a daily challenge. As one of the doctors interviewed in the film describes it, it's like having "a Ferrari brain with bicycle brakes—you can't control it."[1]

Andrés Torres played for the San Francisco Giants from 2009 until he was traded to the New York Mets at the end of 2011. In recent years he has become a spokesperson for ADHD awareness.

> **KIDS WITH "THE FIDGETS"**
>
> *ADHD used to be called* hyperactivity. *The prefix* hyper *means "too much." A hyperactive child is more active than most kids. He or she usually has trouble sitting still. Hyperactive kids often fidget, rock back and forth, or suddenly jump up and run around.*

Many people with attention disorders have other symptoms as well. Some, like Andrés Torres, are bursting with energy and have difficulty sitting still (hyperactivity), and have trouble controlling their actions (impulsivity). Others have a lack of energy and problems staying focused, signs of a condition called attention deficit disorder, or ADD for short. The term *attention-deficit/hyperactivity disorder (ADHD)* is now used for the whole group of attention disorders. It includes people with or without hyperactivity.

ADHD is a common disorder that affects over 6.4 million school-age children in the United States. ADHD affects about 9 percent of American children ages thirteen to eighteen.

ADHD is a common disorder that affects over 6.4 million school-age children in the United States.[2] According to the National Institute of Mental Health, ADHD affects about 9 percent of American children ages thirteen to eighteen, and most kids with the disorder are diagnosed by age seven.[3] Not all children with ADHD will grow out of this condition as they get older. In fact, a lot of kids with ADHD—as many as 60 percent—continue to show symptoms as teenagers and adults.[4]

Life in Overdrive

Students with ADHD often have difficulty focusing during classroom lectures.

HYPERFOCUS

How is it that a child diagnosed with an attention-deficit disorder can spend an hour watching a snail make its way slowly across a leaf? One surprising trait that people with ADHD may exhibit is called hyperfocus—the ability to concentrate deeply for long periods of time on something that interests them. They might play a video game for hours, totally oblivious to the world around them. They have trouble regulating their attention, however. They can't easily shift gears to focus on necessary but less interesting tasks. Some people see hyperfocus as a positive feature of ADHD. A person who can concentrate for hours on something productive such as a difficult mechanical problem might grow up to become an exceptional engineer.

People with ADHD, whether they are hyperactive or quiet, have a hard time controlling their behavior. Kids may have trouble learning in school, behaving at home, or making and keeping friends. Adults may also have problems with friends and family, and they may not be able to keep a job for very long. As a result, many people with ADHD often feel like they are bad or stupid. The truth is, their brains just work differently from the way most people's do. Fortunately, ADHD can be treated. There are medicines that, when taken daily, can help people sit still and focus better. People can also learn how to control their behavior through behavior therapy (treatment involving techniques to help change behaviors). With proper treatment, people with ADHD can gain control over their lives and feel better about themselves.

Chapter 2

ADHD Throughout History

ADHD is currently one of the most commonly diagnosed neurodevelopmental disorders of childhood. Some people claim that the distractions of modern life, such as cell phones and video games, are to blame for this condition. However, medical historians would argue that ADHD has always existed, though under different names. They could point to an ancient treatise written by the Greek physician Hippocrates (460–370 BCE), often called "the father of medicine." Hippocrates observed patients who demonstrated "quickened responses to sensory experiences" and who had difficulty focusing because "the soul moves on quickly to the next impression."[1]

More than two thousand years after Hippocrates, in 1798, the Scottish-born physician and author Sir Alexander Crichton wrote a medical treatise called "An Inquiry into the Nature and Origin of Mental Derangement" in which he described a condition of mental restlessness and inattention. Crichton noted that the condition could emerge at an early age and that it sometimes diminished over time. Sufferers described what

ADHD Throughout History

Ancient Greek physician Hippocrates was one of the first to describe a disorder similar to what we know as ADHD.

they experienced as "the fidgets," which made it difficult to keep still or to focus on a single subject.[2]

German psychiatrist Heinrich Hoffmann became well known when he published a book of rhymed stories called *Der Struwwelpeter* (or *Shockheaded Peter*), which he wrote and illustrated for children in 1845. His strange stories described children who misbehave, most likely based on his observations of young patients he had treated.

An illustration from Heinrich Hoffmann's *Der Struwwelpeter* (*Shockheaded Peter*). Hoffmann's book about misbehaving children included a story about a boy who may have been diagnosed with ADHD today.

Today, medical experts believe that Dr. Heinrich Hoffmann's writings of misbehaving children, especially one called "The Story of Fidgety Philip," gave the first accurate description of what we now call attention-deficit/hyperactivity disorder (ADHD).[3]

NEW UNDERSTANDING OF AN OLD PROBLEM

Extremely fidgety, overactive kids have been around since long before the 1800s—probably for as long as children have been around. And throughout history, kids who "misbehaved" were often treated very badly. Most of the misbehaving children depicted in Hoffman's book suffer a gruesome fate. Centuries ago, many people believed that hyperactive behavior was caused by demons taking over a person's body—or else it was a punishment by the gods. Well into modern times, it was commonly believed that a child's unacceptable behavior was simply the result of poor parenting. Too often, these children were punished with severe beatings.

> *ADHD was not formally recognized as a medical condition until the early 1900s.*

While ADHD may have been around a long time, it was not formally recognized as a medical condition until the early 1900s. In 1902 English pediatrician George Still presented a series of lectures to the Royal College of Physicians. He discussed behavior problems in a group of forty-three children he treated in his medical practice. He described these children as defiant, aggressive, resistant to discipline, lawless, overly emotional, passionate, and having little "inhibitory volition" (control of their actions).[4] Basically, these kids had little or no awareness of their destructive behavior. Most of the children in this were boys, and the alarming behaviors were noticeable before the age of eight.

THE STORY OF FIDGETY PHILIP

"Let me see if Philip can
Be a little gentleman;
Let me see if he is able
To sit still for once at the table."
Thus Papa bade Phil behave;
And Mama looked very grave.
But Fidgety Phil,
He won't sit still;
He wriggles,
And giggles,
And then, I declare,
Swings backwards and forwards,
And tilts up his chair,
Just like any rocking horse—
"Philip! I am getting cross!"
See the naughty, restless child
Growing still more rude and wild,
Till his chair falls over quite.
Philip screams with all his might,
Catches at the cloth, but then
That makes matters worse again.
Down upon the ground they fall,
Glasses, plates, knives, forks and all.
How Mama did fret and frown,
When she saw them tumbling down!
And Papa made such a face!

Philip is in sad disgrace....[5]

In 1845 Hoffmann published this story about a boy who cannot sit still.

ADHD Throughout History

For a long time, many people believed that the only way to deal with hyperactive or disruptive children was to punish them, as shown in this 1831 illustration.

Dr. Still was surprised to learn that most of the kids came from "good homes," so it did not seem that their destructive behaviors resulted from bad parenting. He thought that the problem was more biological than it was psychological. He suspected that the condition was either inherited or caused by brain damage at birth. Dr. Still also found out that some of the children's family members had other psychiatric problems such as depression, alcoholism, or conduct problems.

Dr. Still's ideas had a big impact on the medical community. Medical experts started to change their way of thinking. They realized that perhaps these children were not bad or evil. In the years that followed, researchers continued to study this behavioral condition in hopes of finding kinder, more effective methods of treatment.

In the 1920s researchers discovered that a number of children had developed behavior problems after having encephalitis (a viral infection of the brain) during a major outbreak in 1917–1918. These children were hyperactive, lacked control over their actions, and had a very short attention span—the same behavior problems that Dr. Still had described years earlier. Doctors felt that these behaviors were caused by brain damage. Children who showed these symptoms were labeled "brain damaged." Even if they had not had encephalitis, they were still called brain damaged. Eventually, however, doctors realized that many of the children were actually quite smart. How could their brains work so well if they were damaged? There must be some other cause for hyperactive behavior.

METHODS OF TREATMENT

In 1937 American physician Charles Bradley discovered the first effective treatment for ADHD quite by accident. He was trying to find a drug that would ease spinal tap headaches in children. (A spinal tap procedure is a medical test that involves removing fluid from the spinal column. A common side effect is a really bad headache.) He noticed that one drug he tried, Benzedrine, did little to help the headaches, but seemed to calm some of his patients who had behavior problems. In fact, teachers reported that a number of the children showed great improvement in their behavior and learning in the classroom. Some of the kids even called the medication "math pills" because they were having an easier time learning math. (This subject used to be very difficult for them.) When the children stopped taking the medication, however, their teachers noticed that the old behaviors returned.

Dr. Bradley found the results very surprising because Benzedrine is a stimulant—a drug that normally raises the heart rate, blood pressure, and activity level. He did not understand why the stimulant seemed to calm hyperactive children.

ONE DISORDER WITH MANY NAMES

Over the last one hundred years, ADHD has gone through a number of name changes. The name seemed to change whenever researchers learned new information about the condition. When brain damage was believed to be a cause, the condition was called minimal brain damage (MBD), *and later* minimal brain dysfunction. *It has also been commonly called* hyperactivity, *because a telltale sign of the condition is being overactive.*

In 1980 the American Psychiatric Association added the name attention deficit disorder (ADD) *to their official list, to focus on the lack of attention. This could occur either with or without hyperactivity. The name was changed again in 1994 to* attention-deficit/hyperactivity disorder (ADHD), *which was used to describe a condition with inattention, hyperactivity, or a combination of both. Some mental health experts are uncomfortable with the term* disorder *in ADHD, since it suggests that there is something "wrong." They think that the brains of people with ADHD just work differently. Other people object to the term* attention-deficit, *arguing that many individuals with the condition have no difficulty focusing their attention on subjects that interest them. As understanding of the condition evolves, it seems likely that ADHD will go through more name changes in the future.*

What You Can Do About ADHD

Not long ago, students who misbehaved in class were taught that there was something wrong with them and that they were "naughty."

THE SEARCH FOR A CAUSE

Despite Dr. Bradley's promising findings, stimulants were not used much to treat hyperactive children until the 1950s and 1960s. In 1955 the Food and Drug Administration (FDA) approved the stimulant methylphenidate (brand name Ritalin) to treat a number of psychological disorders, which did not yet include ADHD.

In 1960 New York child psychiatrist Stella Chess coined the term *Hyperactive Child Syndrome*. In a research paper, she described a hyperactive child as "one who carries out activities at a higher than normal rate of speed than the average child, or who is constantly in motion, or both."[6] Some of her hyperactive patients had obvious causes for their behavior: brain damage, mental retardation, extreme stress in their environment, or a serious mental illness. But many of them—thirty-seven out of eighty-two—had no past problems other than their hyperactive behavior.[7] Other experts at the time believed that hyperactivity was caused by bad parenting or toxins (poisons) in the environment. Chess, however, felt that hyperactivity was due to something different in the workings of the brain. She recommended a combined approach to treatment, including behavior therapy, medication, special education in the schools, active involvement of the parents, and psychotherapy if the child's hyperactive behavior had resulted in psychological problems.

The research of Chess and others began to change psychiatrists' views of hyperactive children and how they should be treated. By 1967 Ritalin was being prescribed specifically to treat children with hyperactivity. Using stimulants to treat this condition soon became increasingly common.

The hyperactivity disorder stirred up a lot of controversy. Not everybody could agree on what caused it, let alone how to treat it. In 1973 Dr. Benjamin Feingold, a pediatrician and allergist, proposed a different theory on the cause of hyperactivity. He believed that food additives, preservatives, and

What You Can Do About ADHD

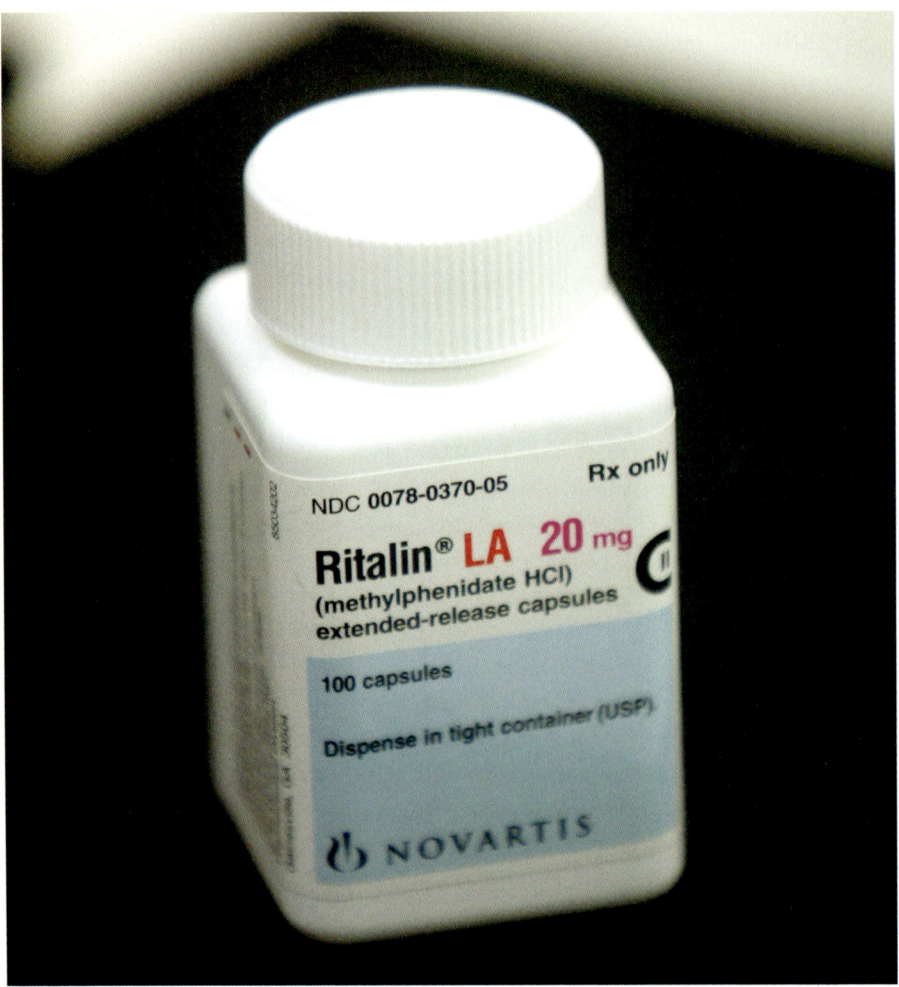

In 1967 Ritalin, a stimulant, began being prescribed for hyperactive children.

artificial colorings were to blame for making kids overactive. He also suggested that eating too much sugar could bring on the condition. He recommended that parents reduce the amount of sugar their children ate. He offered a special diet that did not include food colorings or any other artificial chemicals. He also recommended other foods that contained natural chemicals called salicylates. These substances, chemically related to aspirin, can be found in everyday foods such as almonds, cucumbers, tomatoes, apples, and berries.

Dr. Feingold found that up to 50 percent of children who stuck to his recommended diet showed improvement.[8] Many parents welcomed this new diet as a safe alternative to medication. The National Institute of Mental Health (NIMH) conducted a number of independent studies on the effect of a restricted diet on hyperactivity. In 1982 the NIMH announced that such a diet helped only about 5 percent of hyperactive children—mostly young children with food allergies.[9]

During the 1970s, doctors started to realize that some adults had attention problems, too. Researchers interviewed their parents and childhood teachers and found that the adults in question had shown typical signs of hyperactivity as children, but had gone undiagnosed.

In 1990 NIMH researcher Alan Zametkin and his team conducted a study to find out if the brains of people with ADD worked differently from those of people in the general population. The study team used a positron-emission tomography (PET) scan, in which a radioactive form of glucose (a sugar) was injected into the subjects. (The amount of radiation given to the subjects was very small—not enough to harm them.) On PET scans, areas of the brain that are working actively take up the radioactive sugar and show up as bright spots. Scans were taken of adults with attention problems and a similar group without any symptoms of ADD. The brain scans of the two groups looked quite different. In people without attention

What You Can Do About ADHD

In the 1970s, it was widely believed that sugar and artificial coloring could cause ADHD. This idea was later disproved.

problems, certain areas in the scan were brightly lit, but in those with ADD symptoms, the same areas showed up as dim or dark. For example, there was less brain activity in the frontal lobe (in the forehead) in people with ADD. The frontal lobe of the brain is involved in attention and self-control. Many medical experts felt that these findings indicated that ADD was indeed a medical condition.

In 1999 the *American Journal of Psychiatry* published the results of the largest study on ADHD treatment in history. It was called the *Multimodal Treatment Study of Children with ADHD*, or *MTA* for short. This study, sponsored by NIMH, went on for fourteen months and involved nearly six hundred schoolchildren, aged seven to nine, diagnosed with ADHD. The purpose of the study was to find out which type of ADHD treatment was most effective: 1) medication alone,

2) behavioral treatment alone, 3) a combination of both, or 4) routine community care. The last group allowed parents to decide which treatments were best for their children. Most of the children in this group received medication prescribed by their family doctors. Typically, these children received lower doses of drugs such as Ritalin than those in group one.

Early findings showed that either medication alone or a combination of medication with behavioral treatment (groups one and three) were much more effective in reducing ADHD symptoms than strictly behavioral treatments alone or community care. A rather surprising result was that the children treated with medication (alone or with behavioral treatment) improved greatly in social situations as well. They cooperated better with their parents and classmates. The researchers concluded that treating ADHD eliminated the symptoms that

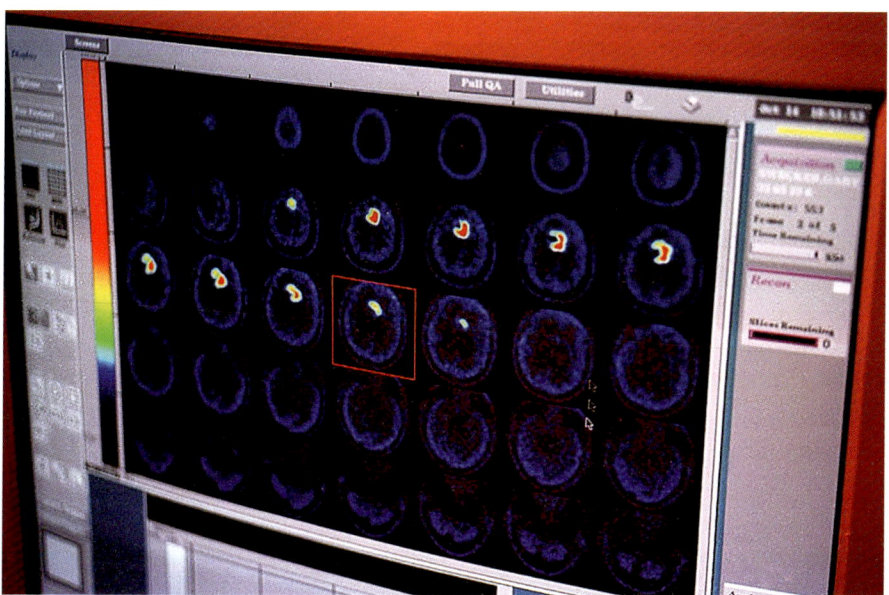

PET scans show activity in the different areas of the brain. Researchers have learned that there is a difference in the brain activity of those with ADHD and those without it.

had kept children from learning social skills. Researchers continued to publish follow-up reports in the following years based on this large study. They observed the children through adolescence to track long-term effects of the early treatment.[10]

3 Chapter

UNDERSTANDING ADHD

D av (pronounced Dave) Pilkey is the author and illustrator of popular children's books, including the Captain Underpants and Super Diaper Baby series. He knows exactly how to get kids excited about reading. What kid could resist potty humor and booger jokes in such books as *Captain Underpants and the Attack of the Talking Toilets*? But Dav's books are more than just silly bathroom humor—kids can really relate to them. The mischievous main characters of the Captain Underpants books, George Beard and Harold Hutchins, do rather poorly in school, and they often find themselves getting into trouble with their teachers and school principal. Their adventures are more than just stories; they are actually based on Dav's own experiences growing up. When he was young, Dav Pilkey was diagnosed with attention-deficit/hyperactivity disorder.

Dav Pilkey has loved to draw for almost his entire life. As a little kid, he spent a lot of time drawing animals, monsters, and superheroes. When Dav started kindergarten, he learned how much fun it was to make people laugh. He was really good at

What You Can Do About ADHD

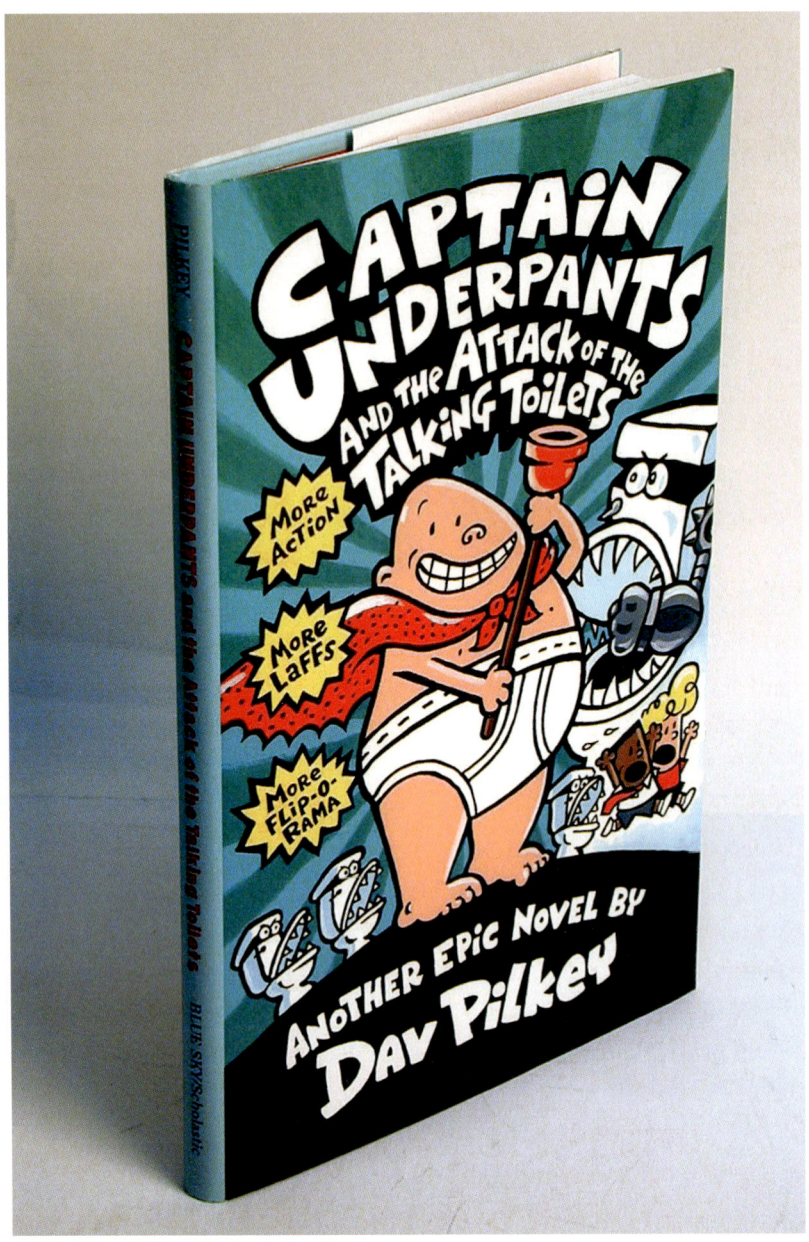

Dav Pilkey, author of the Captain Underpants series, struggled with paying attention when he was in school. He was eventually diagnosed with ADHD.

making funny noises and seeing how many crayons he could stick up his nose. Unfortunately, his teacher didn't think he was very amusing. She found him disruptive and sent him to the principal's office on a regular basis. He spent so much time in the principal's office that his parents finally had to seek professional help to find out why Dav couldn't behave in school. It was then that Dav was diagnosed with learning and reading problems, as well as ADHD.

Dav continued to have a tough time in school. In first grade, he was known as a class clown. His teacher didn't like his kind of humor, so she often sent him out of the classroom. Eventually, she moved a desk out into the hallway for him. Dav used this time to make his own little comic books from a supply of paper, pencils, and crayons that he had stuffed into the hallway desk before class. One of the characters he created was Captain Underpants. Everybody in his class loved his silly superhero—except for his teacher. One day, she ripped up one of his books and told him that he needed to take life more seriously, rather than spending his time making "silly books." He didn't listen to her, though.

High school was not much better for Dav. His teachers did not encourage his artistic talents. Things changed in college, though. One of Dav's professors told him that she liked his creative writing skills, and she encouraged him to write books. This is when Dav wrote his first book, *World War Won*, which won a contest and later got published.[1]

Through his books, Dav tries to encourage kids who struggle in school like he did. "I try to get the point across that not everybody thinks the same way," he explains. "Try to remember that being unsuccessful in school doesn't automatically mean you'll be unsuccessful in life. Lots of people who didn't excel in school still went on to have successful lives. For example, Thomas Edison's teachers thought he was retarded . . . but he ended up doing pretty well for himself."[2]

What You Can Do About ADHD

Dav Pilkey meets a young fan at the Texas Book Festival.

Understanding ADHD

HIGHLY SUCCESSFUL PEOPLE WITH ADHD

Many people with ADHD are very smart and creative. They have become teachers, doctors, lawyers, inventors, movie stars, company presidents, or athletes. Although the condition may not have been officially diagnosed, some historians and psychologists believe that a number of famous people—past and present—have had ADHD. They base this view on studies of their behavior patterns.

Name	Occupation
Alexander Graham Bell	Inventor
Ludwig van Beethoven	Composer
Terry Bradshaw	Football player/sports analyst
Jim Carrey	Actor/comedian
Cher	Singer/actress
Walt Disney	Cartoonist
Thomas Edison	Inventor
Albert Einstein	Physicist
Dwight D. Eisenhower	General, U.S. president
Benjamin Franklin	Politician, inventor, scientist
Cammi Granata	Hockey player
Dustin Hoffman	Actor
Wolfgang Amadeus Mozart	Composer
Howie Mandel	Comedian/TV personality (America's Got Talent)
Pablo Picasso	Artist
Steven Spielberg	Filmmaker
Robin Williams	Actor/comedian

What You Can Do About ADHD

Comedian Jim Carrey was diagnosed with ADHD as a young boy. His teachers used to complain that he disrupted the rest of the class.

BEHAVIORAL ISSUES

ADHD is a condition in which people have trouble controlling their behavior in different settings, such as at home or in school. All children have behavior problems at times. Children with ADHD have problems that are extreme and occur more often than in most children.

People who have ADHD may sometimes seem like they are "spaced out"—they don't seem to listen to what is said. Sometimes they may seem unfriendly, strange, too talkative, or mean. That is why some kids with ADHD have trouble making and keeping friends. They are often fun to be around because they have a lot of imaginative ideas and a great sense of humor, but it can be hard to spend a lot of time with them.

Attention-deficit/hyperactivity disorder, or ADHD for short, is a condition in which people have trouble controlling their behavior in different settings, such as at home or in school.

Kids with ADHD may also have trouble getting along with their own family. They may not listen to their parents, or they may fight with their siblings all the time. In school, teachers find them disruptive and may think they are not very smart. Actually, most children with ADHD have at least average intelligence or higher. However, one in four kids with ADHD will also have a specific type of learning problem and will often do poorly in school.[3] These students do have the ability to learn, but many of them have trouble focusing long enough to do their schoolwork. They may have difficulty taking tests or doing long writing assignments, so they get poor grades.

Eventually, kids with ADHD may feel as though they can no longer relate to the people in their lives. This can make them feel sad and lonely. They don't feel good about themselves, and

What You Can Do About ADHD

WHAT A BORE!

Everybody gets bored sometimes. It's no surprise if your mind wanders while you are sitting on a bench waiting for your turn to play ball, or reading a chapter in a textbook. People with ADHD, however, have a lot of trouble dealing with boredom. They feel a need to be constantly doing something, and they begin to fidget when they have to sit still. That is why it is often difficult for kids with ADHD to be calm and attentive when they need to—for example, when sitting quietly during a classroom lecture. Adults with ADHD can become so distracted in boring situations that they fail to do their jobs properly.

People with ADHD have a hard time dealing with boredom. They might act out if forced to sit still for too long.

they may develop low self-esteem. Kids with ADHD really do want to get along with their friends, family, and teachers, but they do not realize when they are saying or doing something inappropriate. Often they are surprised when their behaviors upset or annoy other people.

WHO IS AT RISK FOR ADHD?

Children as young as three years old may show symptoms of ADHD, but their parents may think they just have a lot of energy. The symptoms are likely to be noticed around school age, when kids are expected to follow rules and control their behavior. Seven is the average age that most children with ADHD receive a diagnosis.

For many years, scientists believed that only children have ADHD. They thought kids just "grew out of it" before they became adults. They now know that this is not always true.

Adults with ADHD are not usually hyperactive. That may be why doctors used to think that kids grow out of it. Adults with ADHD often have trouble paying attention and may act quickly, without thinking. They may also have trouble with relationships and have a hard time finishing projects. They may have low self-esteem, just like kids with ADHD, because they have trouble controlling their behavior.

People with ADHD often have family members—parents, grandparents, aunts, uncles, brothers or sisters, or cousins—who also have ADHD.

THREE TYPES OF ADHD

Not everyone with ADHD behaves the same way. In fact, ADHD symptoms can vary a great deal. Some people are full of energy and can't sit still. Others are calm, but they can't concentrate and have trouble paying attention. Symptoms also present differently in boys and girls. That's why experts often talk about

What You Can Do About ADHD

TRAPPED IN A PINBALL MACHINE

If you don't have ADHD, try to imagine what it feels like. First, turn on the TV and the radio. Then ask a friend to talk to you. While all this is going on, sit down and try to do your homework. Can you tune out all the distractions and do your homework? Can you talk to your friend without paying attention to the TV or radio? Some people with ADHD have trouble sorting out the many sounds, sights, and thoughts that demand attention. They do not know how to focus on just one thing at a time and tune out the rest. One person with ADHD described how it felt when he tried to do something as simple as read a book: "My thoughts raced round and round in my head. It's like my mind was a pinball machine with five or six balls smashing into each other."[4]

Understanding ADHD

Michelle Suppers did not receive her ADHD diagnosis until she was an adult. She saw similarities between herself and her older son, who also has ADHD.

three kinds of ADHD: hyperactive-impulsive type, inattentive type, and combined type.

> *Not everyone with ADHD behaves the same way. In fact, ADHD symptoms can vary a great deal. Some people are full of energy and can't sit still. Others are calm, but they can't concentrate and have trouble paying attention.*

Hyperactive-impulsive type. Hyperactive kids are full of energy and always seem to be on the go. They are often fidgety and squirm in their seats. They may run around, touching or playing with whatever they see. They may have a hard time sitting still for a story or during a classroom lesson. They may talk constantly when they are supposed to be listening. Hyperactive teenagers and adults are not as obvious as kids. They may feel restless on the inside. They often need to keep themselves busy and try to do several things at once.

Impulsive kids do not always think before they speak or act. They often blurt out things that are inappropriate, such as commenting negatively on how someone looks. They also have trouble waiting their turn, such as during a game. They may frequently interrupt other people. They may grab a toy from another child or start hitting when they don't get what they want right away. Impulsive teenagers and adults may also act quickly and without thinking. While driving, for example, they may zip through traffic, weaving from lane to lane. They may stop suddenly or turn without signaling beforehand. They react without thinking about the effects their actions might have on other people.

Inattentive type. This type is often called attention deficit disorder (ADD). People with ADD have trouble paying attention. Their minds are often filled with so many thoughts and ideas that it is hard for them to concentrate on any one thing.

Understanding ADHD

Children who are hyperactive feel the need to be moving or talking constantly. They have a hard time settling down.

BASEBALL AND ADHD

Statistics released in 2012 by Major League Baseball (MLB) showed that the rate of ADHD among professional ball players was twice as high as in the general population.[5] Some people worried that certain athletes were taking advantage of a rule allowing prescription stimulant use for players diagnosed with ADHD. In the history of this highly competitive sport, many professional athletes have resorted to taking performance-enhancing drugs such as steroids. Policies banning such drugs are strictly enforced, and drugs tests are routinely administered, but the sport has witnessed many "doping" scandals. Was the epidemic of ADHD in baseball more evidence of this cheating?

Individuals with ADHD often gravitate toward sports because it helps them to focus and builds self-esteem. That might explain the high incidence of ADHD in the MLB. Professional baseball players must pay attention to many things happening simultaneously on the field in an atmosphere of screaming fans, blaring music, colorful dancing mascots, and huge, flashing screens. Prescribed stimulants such as Adderall and Ritalin can help improve energy and focus in individuals with various types of attention disorders. In any case, baseball officials responded by tightening the rules for granting exceptions for stimulant use for players diagnosed with ADHD. Now a player seeking the exemption needs the approval of a three-expert panel.

They may get bored with a task after just a few minutes and start thinking about something else. Sometimes, though, if they are doing something they like, such as playing video games, they may not have any trouble paying attention. However, they may find it difficult to organize and complete a task or to focus on learning something new.

Kids with ADD are rarely hyperactive or impulsive, yet they also have trouble learning in school. They are too busy daydreaming and often seem spaced out. They may sit quietly and seem to be working, but they are easily confused and may have trouble understanding what they are supposed to do. They find it hard to keep track of things and become distracted easily. They often forget to write down homework assignments, or they leave the assignment at school. They might forget to bring their schoolbook home, or they'll bring home the wrong one. Doing homework is especially difficult. Since people with ADD have a hard time focusing, they often make careless mistakes and have trouble finishing projects. When their homework is finally completed, it is full of errors. The same thing happens when they take tests.

Kids with ADD seem to get along better with friends, family, and teachers than those with hyperactivity and impulsivity do. For this reason, their condition often goes undiagnosed.

Combined type. Some people with ADHD show both inattentive and hyperactive-impulsive symptoms. They are easily distracted and have trouble finishing projects. They are also fidgety and impulsive. Their behavior may change from day to day—they may be quiet and dreamy one day and bubbling over with energy the next.

CAUSES AND RISK FACTORS FOR ADHD

Scientists have learned a lot about ADHD since the 1960s. They know it is not caused by poor parenting or teaching. Many people still think that eating too much sugar can make

MORE BOYS THAN GIRLS

Boys are up to three times more likely to be diagnosed with ADHD than girls, but that doesn't mean the condition is rare in girls. Boys and girls with the disorder display very different symptoms. Boys' ADHD symptoms tend to be more obvious and external. They attract more attention because they are bursting with energy and frequently get into trouble at school. They are impulsive and "act out" more often, and are more physically aggressive than girls. Girls' ADHD symptoms are more likely to go unnoticed because they are less obvious and more "internal." They may daydream in class, feel anxious, and exhibit low self-esteem. They also may try harder than boys to cover up their symptoms. They may spend extra time on schoolwork or ask a parent for help. If they are hyperactive, girls typically express their extra energy in different ways from boys. For example, they may engage in teasing, taunting, and name-calling rather than physical aggression.[6]

Understanding ADHD

kids hyperactive. However, studies have shown that most cases of ADHD are not caused by a high-sugar diet. (Eating a high-protein breakfast instead of sugary foods, on the other hand, has been found to help the brains of kids with ADHD work better.) Most experts believe that ADHD occurs when part of a person's brain doesn't work as well as it should.

Each part of your brain has a special job to do. The outermost layer of the brain is called the cerebral cortex. You use it to think, remember, and make decisions. You also use it to understand and form words and to control body movements. The cerebral cortex receives messages from your ears, eyes, nose, taste buds, and skin and lets you know what is going on in the world around you.

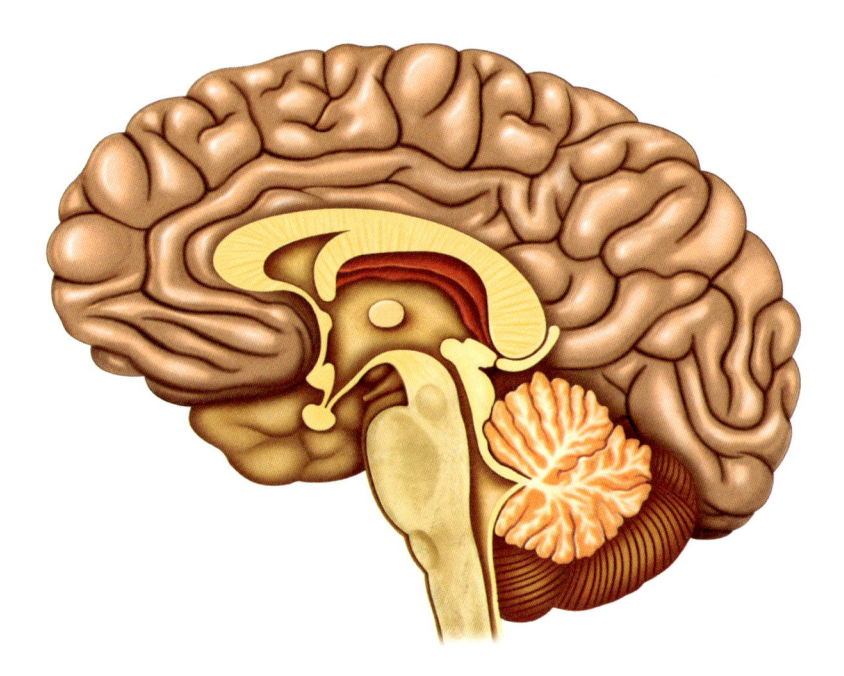

The outer layer of the brain, the cerebral cortex, is responsible for processes like language, attention, and memory.

Most experts believe that ADHD occurs when part of a person's brain doesn't work as well as it should.

Deeper inside the brain there is a kind of relay station that contains billions of nerve cells. These nerve cells receive messages from all over the body and send out messages that control body activities. Chemicals called neurotransmitters help carry these messages from one part of the brain to another. Whenever you concentrate on something—whether it's homework or playing catch with your friends—nerve cells fire off messages back and forth at very high speeds. This fast-paced action makes it possible for you to block out distractions and focus on what you are doing. A healthy balance of neurotransmitters helps to keep the different parts of the brain working properly.

The part of the brain right behind your forehead is called the frontal lobe. It helps you pay attention, focus on one task at a time, make plans and stick to them, and think before you act. In many people with ADHD, some structures in the frontal area are smaller than usual. As a result, the nerve cells in this area can't pick up enough of two important neurotransmitters known as dopamine and norepinephrine. At the same time, some nerve cells grab the neurotransmitters before they reach the places where they are needed.

Low levels of important neurotransmitters— dopamine and norepinephrine—may explain the main types of ADHD behaviors.

Norepinephrine helps a person block out distractions and focus his or her attention. When too little norepinephrine is moving through the brain, a person has trouble focusing on one thing. Dopamine helps people control their actions. If too little dopamine is flowing through the brain, a person may act

Understanding ADHD

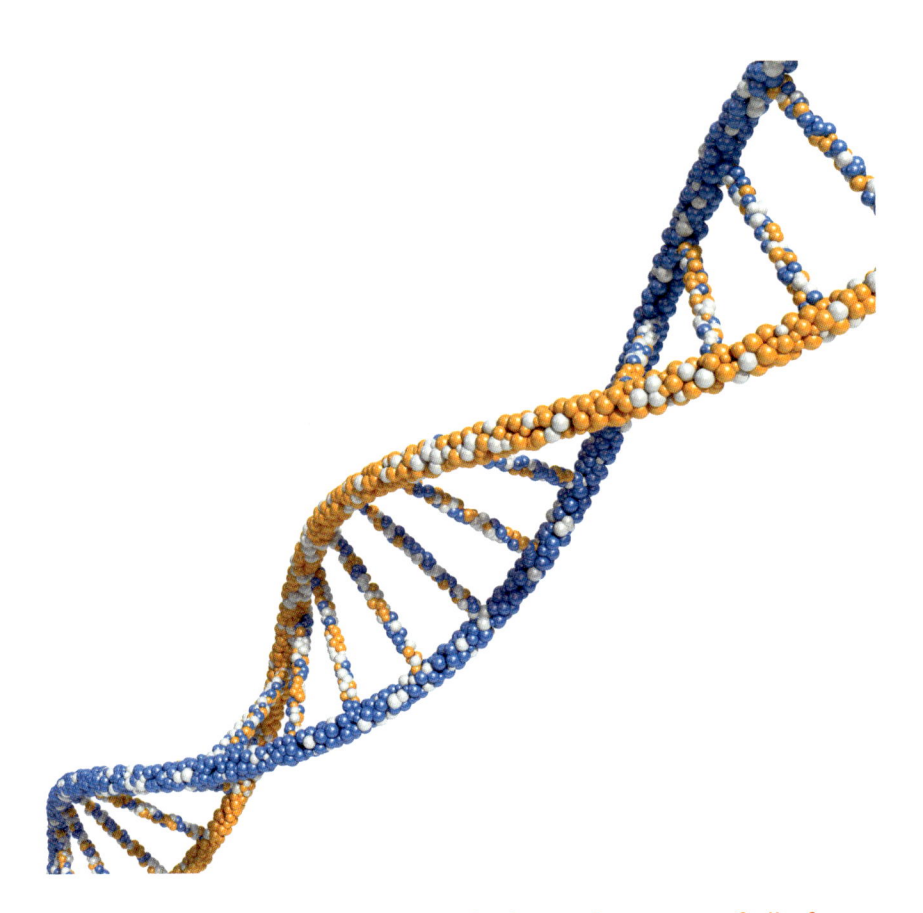

Strands of DNA contain genes, which are the source of all of our inherited traits. ADHD can be passed from parent to child through DNA.

impulsively—shouting out, grabbing things, or even poking a stranger who walks by. Low levels of these important neurotransmitters may thus explain the main types of ADHD behaviors.

Why does this happen? No one knows for sure, but scientists believe that ADHD is inherited—people are born with the condition. The way the brain works is determined by genes, similar to the genes that control inherited traits such as eye color and height. In people with ADHD, the genes that control the way the brain uses neurotransmitters do not work in the same way as they do in other people. Researchers have found, for example, that many people with ADHD have a particular gene for dopamine receptors in their brain cells. (Receptors are chemicals on the cell surface that pick up neurotransmitters and other chemicals.) In such people, some of the nerve cells in the frontal area of the brain, which control behavior, cannot pick up enough dopamine. The amounts of norepinephrine may also vary. Too much norepinephrine can make a person hyperactive; with too little, a person has trouble focusing on one thing at a time.

> **Scientists believe that ADHD is inherited—people are born with the condition.**

Researchers who studied identical twins—siblings who share the exact same genes—were able to show a strong link between genes and ADHD. They found that a child whose identical twin has ADHD has a much greater chance of having ADHD than does a non-twin brother or sister.

A small number of ADHD cases have been linked to other possible causes. For example, a mother who drinks alcohol, smokes cigarettes, or takes drugs during her pregnancy may damage the developing brain of an unborn child. During this time, nerve cells are making important connections, and harmful

Understanding ADHD

CO-EXISTING CONDITIONS

As if ADHD weren't enough to handle, about two-thirds of kids with ADHD have other difficulties, as well, called co-existing conditions. These conditions may affect mood, behavior, and learning in school. Some of the most common ones include the following:

- Learning disabilities. *Some children with ADHD have additional problems with reading, writing, grammar, and/or mathematics.*

- Depression. *These children may feel stupid, isolated, and have low self-esteem because of their problems at school, at home, and with friends.*

- Anxiety. *These children worry a lot and have an overwhelming sense of fear or panic. Anxiety can lead to physical symptoms, which may include a racing heart, sweating, and stomach pains.*

- Severe behavior problems. *These children (mostly boys) are rebellious, disruptive, stubborn, and lose their temper easily. They often argue with adults and refuse to do as they are told. Some of them are likely to get into trouble at school or with the police. They lie, steal, start fights, or bully other kids. They are aggressive toward people and/or animals, destroy others' property, break into people's cars or homes, or carry or use weapons. They are also more likely to abuse alcohol and illegal drugs.*

substances can interfere with this development. Too much alcohol during pregnancy may cause fetal alcohol syndrome (FAS), a condition that can lead to a low weight at birth and mental and physical defects. Many children with FAS are hyperactive, impulsive, and have difficulty paying attention, much like children with ADHD. Toxins (poisons) in the environment, such as the lead in the paint used in old buildings, have been found to cause ADHD symptoms in a few cases. Industrial chemicals, such as PCBs, can be harmful as well. (PCBs are commonly found in water and air pollution.)

Chapter 4

DIAGNOSING AND TREATING ADHD

Molly Zametkin describes herself as the "poster child for female ADHD." When she was in the first grade, her parents and teachers became worried about her behavior in school. She wasn't hyperactive, disruptive, or out of control. Actually, she was quite the opposite: quiet and often distracted. In a student evaluation requested by Molly's parents, her teacher wrote: "Her mind seems to wander in the middle of a task and during instruction. Molly is easily distracted during math—particularly when [working] in small groups."[1] Molly's father recognized the signs of attention deficit disorder (ADD). A well-known research psychiatrist at the National Institute of Mental Health (NIMH), Dr. Alan Zametkin had years of experience identifying the symptoms in other children. However, Molly refused to believe that *she* had ADD. She didn't want to become just another one of her dad's "mental patients."[2]

At first, Molly's parents tried to treat her symptoms with behavior modification, using techniques that help to change behaviors. For some time, Molly refused to take any medication. She felt that would be like admitting she had the disorder. At the end of third grade, when Molly was still having attention problems, her parents took her to see a psychiatrist. He prescribed Dexedrine, a stimulant drug. Molly's work in school improved. Her parents and teachers noticed that she seemed to be more focused and less distractible. Molly herself was still fighting the ADD label, refusing to admit that she had a medical problem.

It wasn't until her freshman year of high school that Molly finally started to accept her diagnosis. Her high school schedule was packed with classes, and after school she had two hours of lacrosse or field hockey practice. After the long days, she still had to do two to three hours of homework. She started to become more aware of her behavior, noticing that sometimes she had a lot of trouble paying attention in her afternoon classes. She worked hard despite her challenges. By the end of the school year, she was happy to see that she had done well in her classes.

Until her sophomore year of high school, Molly did not tell anybody about her ADD. She didn't want anyone to feel uncomfortable hanging out with her, knowing that she needed medication to help her pay attention. Then one day, Molly found out that her friend Jenny (not her real name) also had ADD. Jenny told Molly that she was not playing her best in field hockey practice because she had forgotten to take her Adderall that day. (Adderall is a different stimulant used to treat ADD.) Jenny told Molly that since she had started taking Adderall a few months before, she noticed that her grades and attention level were better than they had ever been.

Molly was surprised to see how Jenny's friends seemed to accept Jenny even after they found out about her condition. She thought that maybe her friends would feel the same way about her. She decided to tell them that she had ADD. Meanwhile, Molly's doctor switched her medication to Adderall. From that

Diagnosing and Treating ADHD

People with ADD do not have hyperactive tendencies. They are easily distracted, have trouble focusing, and may seem to daydream a lot

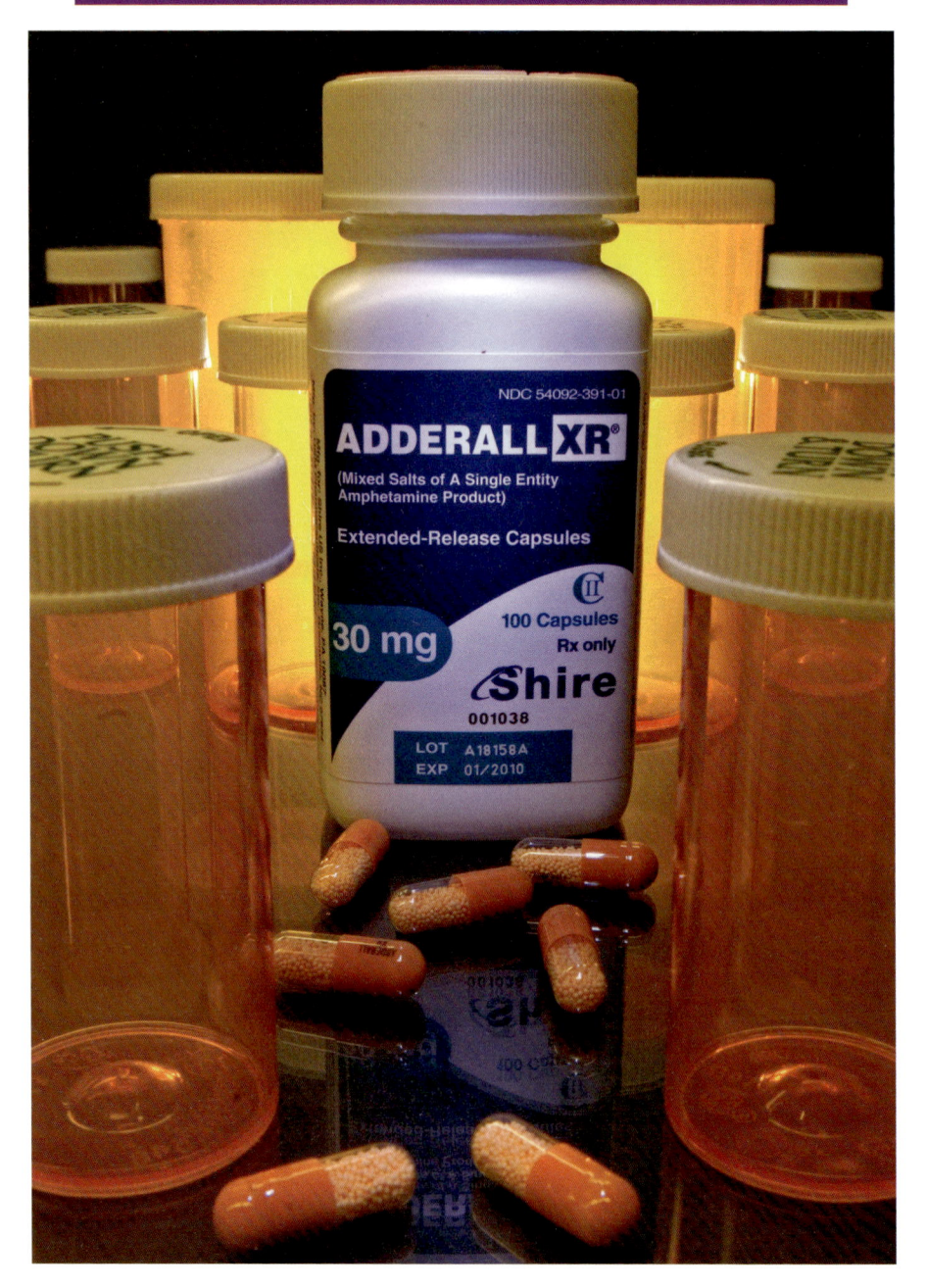

The stimulant Adderall has helped many people with ADHD to have greater focus.

point on, everything changed. She changed her attitude about school. She changed her study habits and followed techniques to get better organized. She started doing homework as soon as it was assigned rather than waiting until the last minute. She took a lot more notes and was able to focus better than she ever had. She also started to exercise and got into good physical shape. Molly's parents were very proud of the progress that she had made. In high school she had four straight years on the honor roll. And when she graduated, her grade point average was 3.9 out of 4.[3]

Molly went on to earn an undergraduate degree in psychology. Today, she works full time at the National Institute on Alcohol Abuse and Alcoholism. She no longer takes medication. With the help of coffee, to-do lists, and compulsive organization, she manages to keep her symptoms at bay and her busy life on track.

WHAT'S NORMAL AND WHAT'S ADHD?

Everybody is hyperactive, impulsive, or inattentive from time to time. That doesn't mean that they have ADHD. There are times when people blurt out things they didn't mean to say, start a new task before finishing an old one, or become disorganized and forgetful. Who hasn't had these things happen to them at one time or another? So how do specialists know whether a person has ADHD or is just energetic?

As of now, there is no actual test that can diagnose ADHD. High-tech brain scans, such as MRI and PET scans, can give a view of the working parts of the brain. Such scans can detect differences in brain activity, and researchers have identified some key differences in the scans of patients with ADHD. However, they cannot yet determine whether or not a person has ADHD from such scans. Changes in brain activity may be signs of other brain disorders. Therefore, brain scans are not widely used as a diagnostic tool at the current time. For

AN ADHD EPIDEMIC?

In the United States, ADHD has become so common that many people think the condition is being overdiagnosed. Some point to the aggressive marketing of ADHD medications for children and, increasingly, for adults, by pharmaceutical companies. Others see a troubling correlation between rising rates of ADHD, especially in the nation's poorest areas, and an increasing push for improved performance in the nation's schools.[4] However, some medical experts do not agree that the condition is overdiagnosed. They say that because scientists have learned a lot about ADHD in recent years, doctors are now better able to identify it. While some cases may be misdiagnosed, many cases actually go undiagnosed. People who have ADD—without the hyperactivity—often go unnoticed because they are quietly daydreaming in the classroom. Many of them are girls like Molly Zametkin. Molly's condition might have gone undiagnosed for many years if her father had not been an expert in identifying the symptoms.

children and teenagers, a diagnosis must be based on symptoms observed by parents, teachers, and a school counselor or mental health professional. Adults often seek help on their own because they are having problems in their work or their relationships with other people.

> *Everybody is hyperactive, impulsive, or inattentive from time to time. That doesn't mean that they have ADHD.*

In many cases, a primary care doctor can make a diagnosis. A physical exam is usually a good way to start. Tests for hearing and vision may be given as well, to rule out other medical conditions. The doctor will also ask a lot of questions. What is the patient's medical history? Does the patient get along well with other people? How does he or she behave at home and at school or work? How long has the patient been behaving this way? How does the patient's behavior cause trouble? It is important to make sure that the behaviors are not linked to problems at home. For example, children who have experienced a serious life event, such as a divorce, a move, an illness, a change in school, or a death in the family, may act out or become forgetful.

If the doctor suspects ADHD, he or she may recommend that the patient see a counselor, or a mental health specialist such as a psychiatrist or psychologist. The specialist will ask more questions, looking for examples of inattentive behavior and hyperactive or impulsive behavior. The patient may be given psychological tests to evaluate memory, attention, and decision making.

Next, for children and teens, their teachers—both past and present—are asked to fill out a standard evaluation form on the patient's behavior in class. The specialist also needs to talk to

What You Can Do About ADHD

If ADHD is suspected, a physical exam can rule out other medical conditions.

the teachers, parents, and anyone else who knows the patient well, such as coaches or babysitters.

For adults, getting additional information about their behavior may be more complicated. The specialist talks with the patient to get a history of the current problem and childhood behavior that might point to ADHD symptoms. The parents can also provide information about the patient's behavior. Memories of conflicts with other children, failure in school, punishments such as detentions, and frequent visits to the principal's office could be signs of ADHD in childhood. If school report cards are available, they may include comments such as "can't sit still," "doesn't pay attention in class," "does not work well in groups," or "not working up to potential." Interviews with people who are close to the patient, such as friends or a spouse, can also be helpful. Often adults with ADHD have problems at work and tend to get into driving accidents.

Here are some guidelines doctors use in diagnosing ADHD:

- ADHD behaviors first appeared before the person was seven years old.
- Behaviors are more serious and happen more often than in other children of the same age.
- Behaviors have continued for at least six months.
- Behaviors have created major difficulties in at least two areas of a person's life, such as school, work, home, or social settings with friends.

If a person has problems at school or work but behaves normally at home and with friends, he or she probably does not have ADHD.

TREATING ADHD WITH DRUGS

When ADHD is mentioned, many people immediately think of Ritalin. Ritalin is a medicine commonly used to treat ADHD.

CHECKLIST FOR DIAGNOSING ADHD IN CHILDREN

Hyperactive/Impulsive Behavior	Inattentive Behavior
Fidgets a lot and has trouble sitting still.	Often daydreams in class.
Blurts out answers in class.	Is easily distracted.
Interrupts friends while they are speaking.	Has trouble remembering the teacher's instructions.
Has trouble waiting his or her turn in games or groups.	Often loses or forgets his or her homework or books.
Always seems to be "on the go." Runs around a lot or climbs on things when he or she is supposed to be sitting.	Makes careless mistakes in schoolwork.
Talks constantly.	Doesn't listen to his or her parents when asked to do a task.

Diagnosing and Treating ADHD

At least 80 percent of children with ADHD are helped by Ritalin and other ADHD medications.[5] These drugs can help adults with ADHD as well.

Ritalin is a stimulant, a drug that usually makes people feel more wide-awake and full of energy. Stimulants do not make people with ADHD more hyper or active, though. Instead, the drug seems to calm them down. It helps them to pay attention and concentrate, so they are not as easily distracted. In people with ADHD, Ritalin makes dopamine more available to the brain cells.

Ritalin belongs to a family of drugs called amphetamines. These drugs are strong stimulants that are available only with a doctor's prescription. They are controlled by strict laws because they are abused by some people who want to get a "high" (feelings of intense happiness and increased energy). When taken

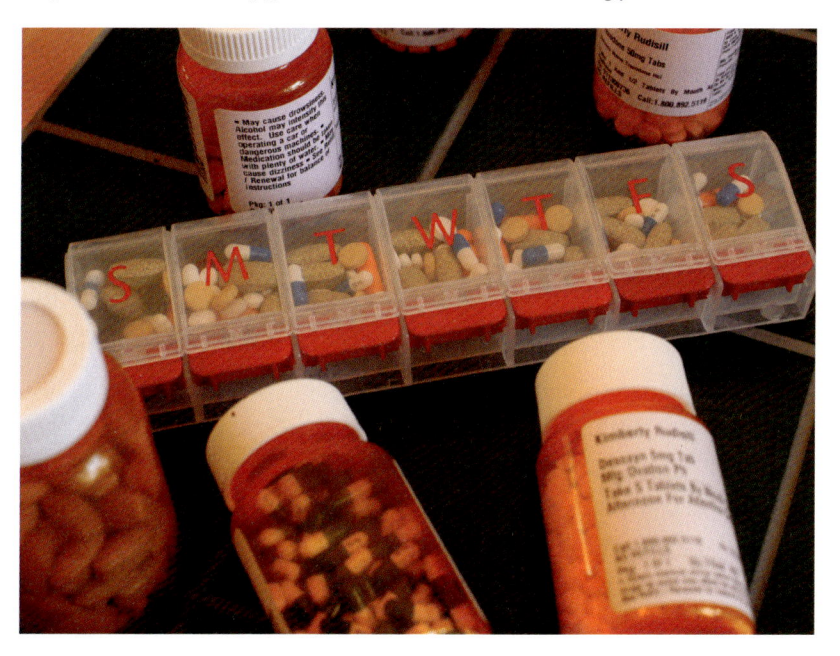

There are many different ADHD medications available today. Each patient, along with a medical doctor, must decide which drug, if any, works best for him or her.

> **HOW SAFE ARE ADHD DRUGS?**
>
> *ADHD medications are safe and effective when taken under a doctor's care. However, stimulants are powerful drugs and they can have negative side effects. Some side effects may be annoying, such as irritability, headaches, increased anxiety, stomachaches, poor appetite, and sleep problems. A high dose of the drug could cause more alarming symptoms, such as increased heart rate and blood pressure, seizures (uncontrollable shaking), damage to the liver, mood changes, confusion, hallucinations, and irregular breathing. Doctors usually start with the lowest dose and then raise it gradually until it is just right. Sometimes a different drug may be more effective for a particular patient. These days, there are a number of ADHD medications from which to choose. Everybody is different. What works for one person may not work for another.*

by people with ADHD, however, these drugs do not produce a high, as long as patients follow their doctor's directions. In 2007 the FDA approved a new amphetamine-type stimulant, Vyvanase, for the treatment of children with ADHD. This drug is less likely to be abused than other amphetamines because it does not produce much of a high.

Many people think that too many children are being treated with ADHD medications. They are frightened by the idea of giving kids a drug that they will take every day for many years. They worry that kids will become addicted to the drugs. However, there is no evidence that ADHD medications, taken in the prescribed doses, lead to drug abuse. In fact, long-term studies have shown that teenagers with ADHD who continued taking their medication through their teen years were less likely to abuse drugs than ADHD teens who were not taking medications.

On the other hand, there are people who think Ritalin is a magic pill that can make ADHD disappear. When parents and

Diagnosing and Treating ADHD

Blake Taylor started taking ADHD medication when he was five years old. At the time of this photo, he was nineteen years old and still taking drugs for ADHD.

teachers notice an improvement in the child's schoolwork and behavior, right away they consider the drug as some kind of cure. However, as yet, there is no cure for ADHD. Medications can only control the symptoms on the day they are taken. If the child forgets to take the medicine, the symptoms will return.

In 2003 the Food and Drug Administration (FDA) approved Strattera (atomoxetine), the first nonstimulant treatment for ADHD. This drug raises the level of norepinephrine in the brain but can also produce serious side effects. Other nonstimulant medications now prescribed for ADHD include guanfacine and clonidine.

Doctors may prescribe antidepressants such as buproprion, to ADHD patients who also suffer from depression. However, these drugs are not as effective as stimulants or Strattera in treating ADHD itself because they do not help to improve a person's attention span or concentration. Some antidepressants may also have dangerous side effects, including an increased risk for suicidal thoughts.

MEDICATED TODDLERS

In May 2014 The New York Times raised concerns when it reported that an estimated ten thousand or more American toddlers were being given medications, including Adderall and Ritalin, to control ADHD-like symptoms.[6] According to Dr. Susanna Visser of the CDC, who presented the data, the trend was most prevalent in children from low-income families covered by Medicaid. Currently, children under four are not covered in the American Academy of Pediatric guidelines pertaining to ADHD. This is partly because hyperactivity and impulsiveness are appropriate behaviors for toddlers. Furthermore, very few studies have looked at stimulant use in young children. Only Adderall has been approved by the FDA for children under six.

> **TREATING ADHD WITH A PATCH**
>
> *In April 2006 the FDA approved the first skin patch to treat ADHD in children ages six to twelve. The ADHD patch, called Daytrana, is designed to be worn on the child's hip for nine hours. It releases the same stimulant that is in Ritalin. If there are any negative side effects, the patch can simply be removed. Currently this treatment is recommended only for children who have trouble swallowing pills or refuse to take them. Other kid-friendly choices include chewable tablets and a grape-flavored liquid.*

SHAPING BEHAVIOR

ADHD drugs help kids to pay attention and complete schoolwork, but they do not teach them how to behave in social situations. Adults with ADHD also need training in life skills, such as organizing their activities and getting along with others. That is why many mental health experts agree that ADHD should be treated with a combination of drugs and therapy. One type of therapy frequently used for people with ADHD is called behavior modification.

Behavior modification is a technique used to change a person's behavior. The parent, teacher, or mental health specialist sets goals for a child with ADHD. The adult then rewards good behavior and either ignores inappropriate behavior or works with the child to correct it. There are three steps in this process.

1. Define the problem. If the problem is restlessness, for example, the child may be unable to sit still during dinner.

2. Set a reasonable goal. At first, it may be too hard for a child with ADHD to sit still until everyone in the family has finished eating. It is a good idea to break up the big goal into little goals that are easier to reach. For example, the child can try sitting still at the table for five minutes, then ten minutes, then fifteen minutes.

3. Work toward the goal. Most kids respond to rewards and consequences. Parents, teachers, and friends should praise the child whenever he or she makes some progress, even if the child does not achieve the goal. This will show that they are proud of the child's progress. Going to the movies or getting an ice cream cone may be used to reward reaching a goal. Discipline is also important. Kids need to know that there are consequences for their behaviors. The child should be told what kind of behavior is not acceptable, and what the consequences will be for those actions. A child who does not follow the rules will have a privilege taken away, such as playing video games or going out with friends. The kinds of rewards and consequences are adjusted as the child gets older.

For adults, a professional coach can help in developing more effective behaviors. Various tricks and props can be used. For example, a large calendar placed where it will be seen first thing in the morning can aid in remembering appointments, assignments, and personal goals. Writing lists and reminder notes is also helpful. Having a special place to keep keys, wallet, bills, and paperwork can save a lot of time and stress from looking for things that are misplaced.

THE BENEFITS OF COUNSELING

Many children and adults with ADHD have low self-esteem. Psychological counseling can help them work through the past experiences that led to the feelings of worthlessness and develop a better self-image.

For treatment to be successful, children with ADHD need the support of their parents, teachers, and school counselors. Counselors can help children and family members learn about ADHD and how to cope with it. They can also talk to the children about their condition and help them feel better about themselves. They can help reduce the child's worries and

Diagnosing and Treating ADHD

Allison, shown here with her mother, has ADHD. Allison's parents implemented a reward system to encourage her to get her homework done.

anxieties. They can also teach the child how to handle specific situations at home, at school, or with friends.

Parents and teachers need to learn about ADHD so that they can understand what the child is going through. The more they know about ADHD, the more they can help kids achieve a positive, happy lifestyle. They can also learn ways to help a child change his or her behavior into something more acceptable.

It is very important for parents and teachers to have a lot of patience and understanding. They also need to work together and let each other know about progress and changes in the child's behavior. Friends and family members can help too. Treatment can be a long, frustrating process, but kids with ADHD usually try hard to get better.

For adults in particular, successful treatment of ADHD symptoms can be life-changing. After years of doing things in certain ways, it might be difficult to adjust to a new way of living. Patients may feel that by acting less impulsively, they have lost part of their personality. The therapist can help ADHD patients to adjust to the changes and encourage them to appreciate the accomplishments that result from better organization.

SCHOOL ACCOMMODATIONS FOR ADHD

In 2004 Joanie Derry sued her son's school in Manatee County, Florida. The boy had been diagnosed with ADHD when he was in kindergarten, and a judge had told the school district to create a special education plan for him. The plan stated that the boy needed a chance to move around during class time, and that physical activity allowed him to get along with less medication. The teachers ignored the plan. In fact, they often punished the boy by keeping him in the classroom during recess and not allowing him to play with the other kids. They went back to court two more times before the school district finally agreed to enforce the special education plan.[7]

Diagnosing and Treating ADHD

Dr. Mary Solanto is the director of the ADHD program at the Mount Sinai School of Medicine. She helps people with ADHD manage all the different aspects of their lives.

Two federal laws require schools to provide extra educational services to students who need them, at no cost to parents. The first of these, the Individuals with Disabilities Act (IDEA), lists thirteen categories of disability. ADHD is not among them. However, an ADHD diagnosis is frequently accompanied by secondary diagnoses of a learning disability or developmental delay, which does meet IDEA criteria. When a student qualifies for IDEA accommodations, school staff and parents will work together to develop an Individualized Education Program, called an IEP. An IEP describes a student's learning problems, lists educational services to be provided, sets goals, and defines exactly how the student's progress will be measured over time.

If a child does not qualify for services under IDEA, he or she may still be eligible for support under the second law, Section 504 of the Rehabilitation Act of 1973. A student whose ability to function in school is substantially limited by ADHD symptoms is entitled to receive Section 504 services. Most of

Leah Hornak, who has ADHD, struggled in school until her parents moved her to another school that was better able to accommodate her needs.

Diagnosing and Treating ADHD

Some accommodations that may help students with ADHD are extended test times and quiet testing areas. This high school student is taking her test in a separate room.

these services involve accommodations in the regular classroom, such as providing short breaks between assignments, allowing more time for exams, and seating the student away from distractions such as windows and doors.

Many schools throughout the country do not have programs specifically for kids with ADHD. Most schools do have programs for children with learning disabilities, however. In some cases students with ADHD are assigned to special classes. In others, kids with learning disabilities take most of their classes with the rest of their peers and just go to special classes several hours a week. Parents who want more help for students with attention problems have to hire tutors to work with them after school. There are also some summer programs and schools that give kids with ADHD the extra help they need.

Chapter 5

LIVING WELL WITH ADHD

By all measures, Robert Jergen is what you would call a very successful person. An associate professor with a PhD in special education, he has published many scholarly articles, won awards, written reports to Congress, given talks all over the country, and has been interviewed by *Time* magazine. He is a happily married man who owns his own home.

Looking at him today, it might be difficult to imagine, but when Robert was a child, his mother used to call him "the little monster" because he was always getting into trouble. He was constantly being scolded by his parents and teachers about something he did wrong. What they didn't realize was that Robert wasn't trying to be bad or naughty—he truly couldn't control his behavior.

As Robert got older, being a constant disappointment caused him to sink into depression a number of times. When he went to college, he turned to alcohol to quiet his "noisy" head. The alcohol helped him concentrate in class and get better grades. It also brought out years of pent-up anger, and after

Living Well With ADHD

People with ADHD who act up are not being intentionally "bad." They are unable to control their behavior.

one out-of-control night in a bar, Robert knew he had to stop drinking. Once the drinking stopped, though, the noise in his head started up again.

After college, Robert got a job teaching adolescents with special needs. He loved working with the kids, but he was miserable dealing with the boring paperwork, long meetings, and coworkers constantly angry at the odd things he did or said. Robert's behavior was gradually becoming even more bizarre. One day, he poked a bald area on his boss's head and yelled, "Bald spot!" These words just popped out of his mouth without his even realizing it.

The turning point in Robert's life came when he was talking to one of his students, Troy. Troy had schizophrenia, and Robert was upset to find out that Troy had stopped taking his medication. Robert told Troy that he could be smart and successful if he took his pills every day. Suddenly it occurred to Robert that maybe there was a drug that could improve *his* life.

Robert went to a number of therapy sessions. He also had a functional MRI test taken. This imaging test showed abnormal brain activity. However, doctors could not determine from the MRI whether he had ADHD. One day, Robert went to a support group meeting for adults with learning difficulties. Someone there described what it felt like to live with ADHD: "My mind is like a wall of television sets, each on a different channel, and I don't have the remote." For the first time, Robert felt that someone could relate to what he was going through. "One second I thought that I was a loser. A freak," he said. "The next moment I knew that I had ADHD. I wasn't alone."[1]

For the next two years, Robert was prescribed various ADHD medications, but he stopped taking them because they caused too many negative side effects. He then decided to come up with his own little tricks to control his condition. He started by keeping a journal that showed when and where he got the most work done. That way he could create an environment that

DISTRACTED DRIVING

Teenagers who have ADHD have more traffic accidents than those without the condition. When it comes to driving, avoiding distractions is very important. That means not driving with a carload of friends, not talking on your cell phone or texting while driving, and not getting distracted by loud music in the car. Driving with an adult in the car, even after getting your license, may also help keep you focused.

While distracted driving is dangerous for anyone, it is particularly risky for someone who has ADHD.

would get rid of distractions and allow him to stay focused. For example, Robert keeps his office dimly lit with just a single bright light shining on his computer. The spotlight on his computer reminds him to pay attention. He plays soft music in the background to block outside distractions so that he can relax and concentrate. He also keeps a laptop nearby with a computer game running. He switches to that for a few seconds if his mind starts to wander. When his mind gets in a fog, he hops on his treadmill until he breaks a sweat. This short burst of exercise usually helps to clear his mind so that he can focus again.

Most important, Robert has a strong support system. He met a very encouraging teacher who helped him a great deal when he went back to school for his PhD. Now his wife reminds him to take a walk when he gets angry or frustrated. This support system has helped to rebuild Robert's self-esteem after years of feeling like a failure.

Robert still cannot control his behavior at times, but he has learned how to make his life more manageable. He has written a book about growing up with ADHD. He has also been developing techniques that he hopes will someday help other people with ADHD manage their condition without medication.[2]

There are a number of things that people with ADHD can do to help them listen better, remember things better, and get things done. In fact, the helpful hints on the following pages are good for anybody who has trouble paying attention at times, forgets things, and is not very organized.

WHAT YOU CAN DO AT HOME

- Write notes to yourself. Colored sticky notes are great because you can stick them anywhere.
- If your mom or dad wants you to do something, ask them to write a note so that you won't forget.
- Use a calendar to keep track of places you have to go. Make sure to check the calendar every morning.
- Try to do tasks right away. If you put them off until later, you might forget about them.

Living Well With ADHD

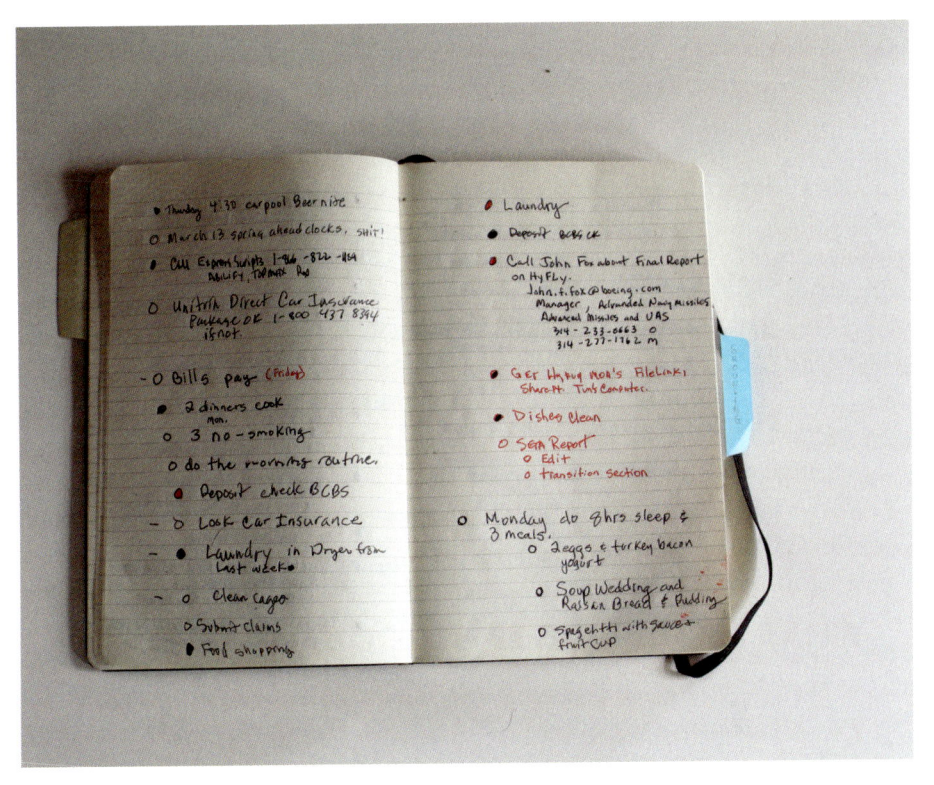

Keeping a journal can be an effective tool for staying organized. This journal belongs to a person with ADHD.

- If you have to go somewhere at a certain time, set the kitchen timer. For instance, if you have to get ready for soccer practice in a half hour, set the timer for thirty minutes

- Do your homework in a quiet place that is away from distractions, such as a TV or siblings. Put your cell phone in another room or shut it off while you are working.

- When you finish your homework, always put your schoolbooks in the same special place so that you won't have to hunt for them in the morning.

- Before you go to bed, decide what clothes you will wear the next day. Place your shoes beside them. That way you won't have to rush around in the morning.

- Develop a morning routine. For example: go to the bathroom, take a shower, get dressed, eat breakfast, brush your teeth, get your books, and go to school.

WHAT YOU CAN DO AT SCHOOL

- Use a student planner. Write down homework assignments and projects, along with their due dates.

- Sit near the front of the classroom, and look at the teacher when he or she is talking.

- Work on one thing at a time. Keep your desk clear of everything else.

- Don't sit next to talkative kids.

- Wear a loose-fitting rubber band on your wrist. If you start to daydream, give it a little snap.

- Keep your phone turned off or put away. It can be a distraction.

Living Well With ADHD

Staying actively engaged in class is one way that a person with ADHD can keep him or herself focused.

- If you don't understand something in class, ask the teacher for help.
- Participate in class. Raise your hand to ask questions and make comments. This will help to make the class more interesting.

HOW TO GET ALONG WITH FRIENDS

- Share your stuff with friends.
- Take turns. Everybody should have a chance to play during a game.
- Stay calm. Don't get overly excited or too loud.
- Before you talk, listen to be sure no one else is already talking. That way, you will not interrupt other people's conversations.
- Compliment your friends when they do something well, and thank them when they help you.
- Don't make fun of other people. They do not like it any more than you do.
- If you feel angry, don't hit, yell, or call names. Walk away and calm down so that you won't say or do something you will feel bad about later.
- Say you're sorry if you have said or done something that hurts someone's feelings.

Chapter 6

Future Directions in Research and Treatment

A biomarker is a measurable indicator of the presence or severity of a disease. For example, a sample of cells taken from a patient's body can help an oncologist make a cancer diagnosis. It can also help the doctor target appropriate treatment for the disease. Diagnosing and treating psychological conditions presents a different challenge, since biomarkers have yet to be identified for these disorders. Until recently, an ADHD diagnosis depended entirely on subjective data—reports from clinicians, therapists, parents, and teaching staff about a child's behavior. Now, computerized diagnostic tools can help doctors make more accurate and objective assessments. Individuals are put through a series of game-like tasks that challenge the brain and test for traits such as sustained attention, inhibition, and impulsivity. One of these programs, called IntegNeuro, has been shown to identify ADHD in young people with 96 percent accuracy.[1]

One day, doctors may be able to diagnose ADHD using a brain scan. In September 2014, American scientists made the discovery that the brains of children and teenagers with ADHD develop more slowly than those without the condition. A research team looked at the brain scans of 275 children and teens with ADHD and 48 without the disorder. They used methods that map the connections between different areas of the brain. The brain scans of the patients with ADHD showed delayed connections between and within key brain networks.[2] This may help explain why people with ADHD are easily distracted and have trouble staying focused.

ALTERNATIVE TREATMENTS

For decades, drugs have been the main focus in treating ADHD. Pharmaceutical treatments work well to control symptoms of the disorder. However, there are concerns over the long-term effects of ADHD drugs. Therefore, people are starting to turn to a variety of alternative treatments such as neurofeedback, electrotherapy stimulation, and working memory training. These methods can be used in addition to the standard treatments. They also provide treatment choices for parents who don't want to give their children drugs and for kids who have had bad reactions to the medications. However, doctors do not yet recommend any of these treatments as proven alternatives to medication and behavioral therapy. Parents of ADHD children and adults with the disorder should be skeptical of any claims that a certain costly therapy provides miraculous benefits and cures ADHD symptoms.

Training the Brain

Neurofeedback is a technique that has been used for years to help improve the concentration of astronauts and Olympic athletes. It is designed to help people train certain parts of their brain. In ADHD, for example, people who have trouble focusing use neurofeedback to change their brain wave patterns in the frontal lobe to increase their concentration.

Future Directions in Research and Treatment

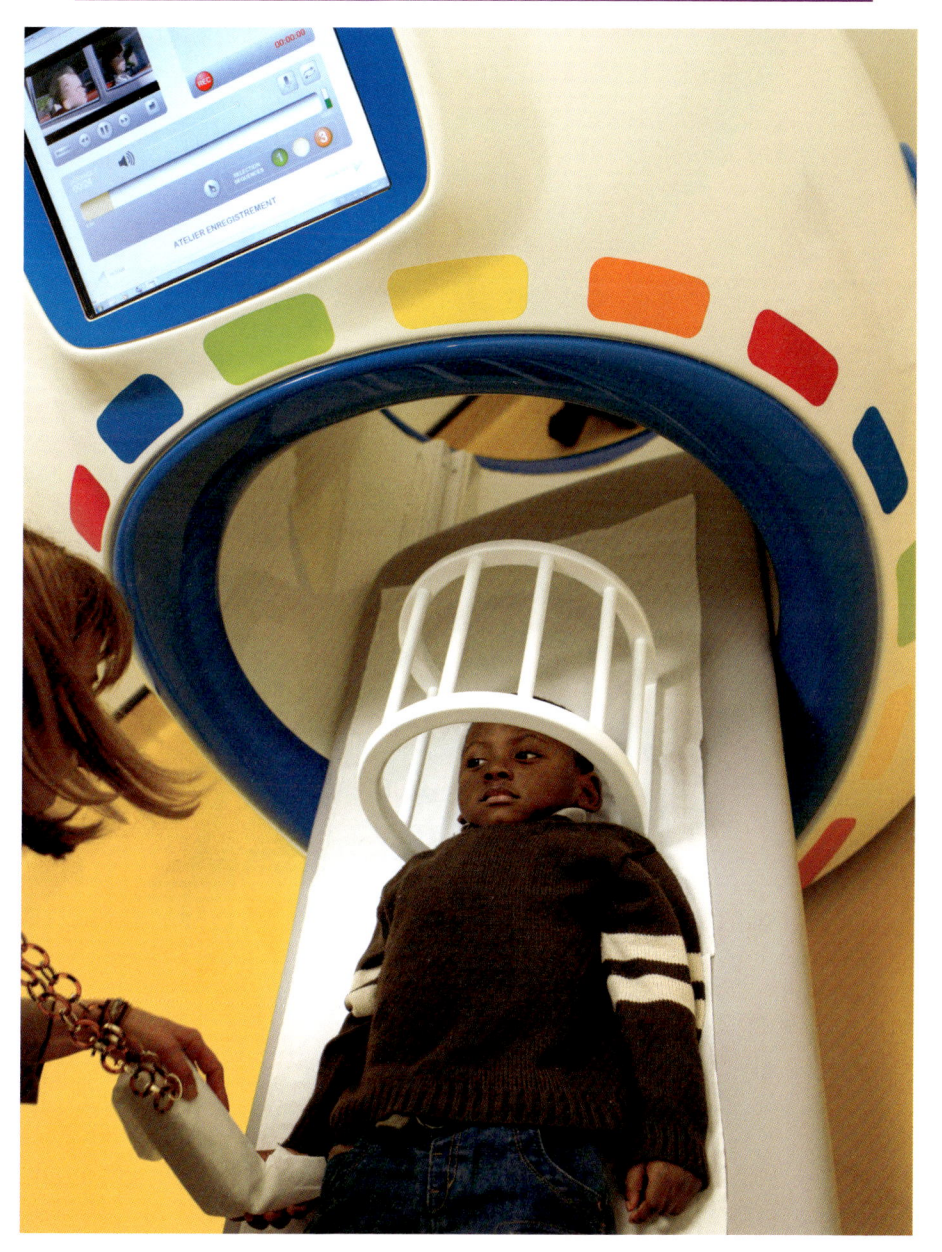

This boy is receiving a brain scan. In the future, doctors may be able to use brain scans to diagnose ADHD.

What You Can Do About ADHD

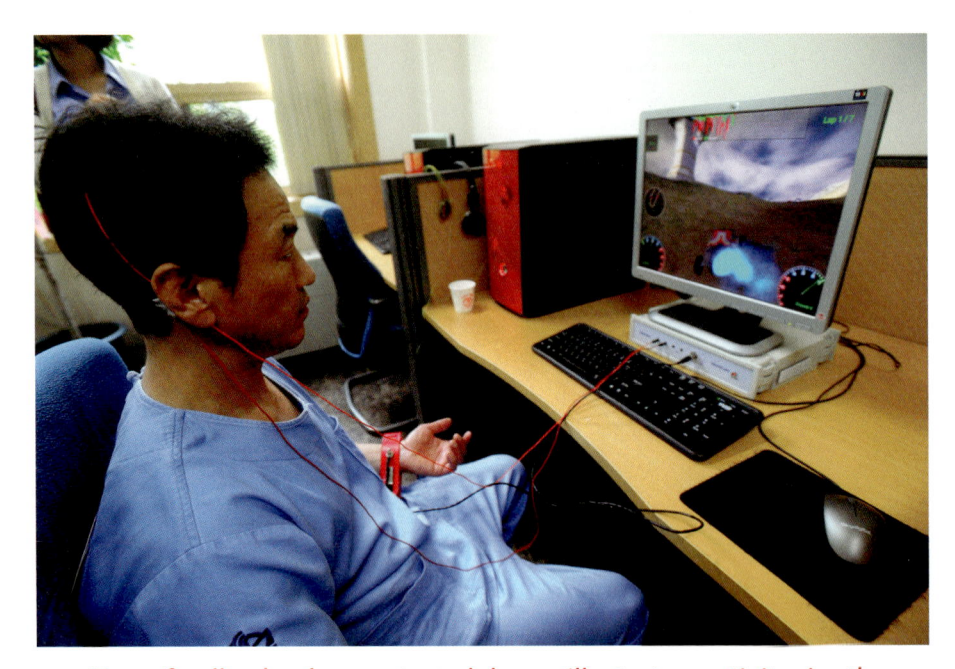

Neurofeedback, demonstrated here, illustrates activity in the brain. Some researchers believe that neurofeedback programs can improve the focus of people with ADHD.

Future Directions in Research and Treatment

How does neurofeedback work? Scientists can determine a person's state of mind by the type of wave pattern in certain parts of the brain. These patterns can be measured and recorded in an electroencephalogram (EEG). There are five main types of brain wave patterns:

- *Beta waves* are the fastest brain waves. A person who is focused has a lot of beta waves.
- *SMR waves* are a type of beta wave. They are observed when a person is mentally preparing for a challenging physical activity. (*SMR* stands for sensorimotor cortex, the part of the brain involved in body senses and muscle movements.)
- *Alpha waves* are slower brain waves. They occur during relaxation.
- *Theta waves* are even slower. They occur when a person is daydreaming or is very close to falling asleep.
- *Delta waves* are the slowest brain waves. They occur when a person is in a deep sleep.

Normally, the amount of beta waves increases when a person tries to concentrate. This doesn't happen in a person with ADHD. Instead, the amount of theta waves—the daydreaming brain wave—increases. Instead of focusing, people with ADHD space out.

The goal of neurofeedback is to train the brain to increase the beta waves in the brain and decrease the theta waves. This therapy uses movies, computers, educational video games, and other tools designed to help patients regulate their own brain waves by rewarding the desired type of brain activity. In a therapist's office, a child with ADHD may sit facing a laptop, playing a computer game. Electrodes attached to the child's

What You Can Do About ADHD

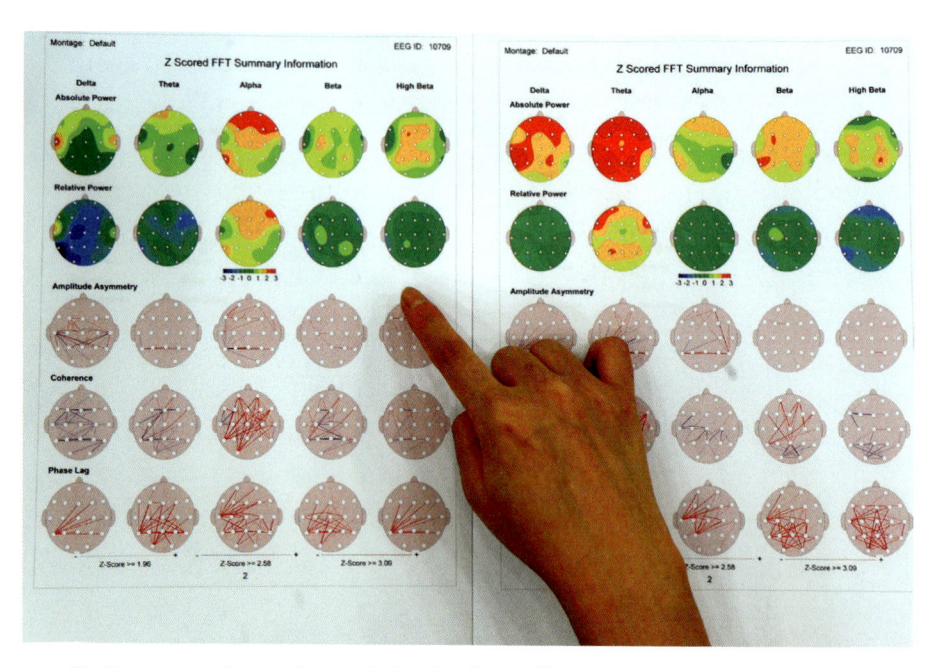

Brain scans show the activity in the different types of brain wave patterns.

scalp monitor her brain activity as she plays, communicating it to the computer with special software. As the gamer's focus improves, the game speeds up or she may earn another type of reward. If she loses focus, the game stops. In one neurofeedback program, a field of flowers bursts into vivid color and birds sing when the patient is focusing well, but when the patient's attention wanders, the flowers wilt and turn gray.

Critics of neurofeedback worry that this type of training hasn't been rigorously tested in large studies as medications have. Lack of hard evidence makes some scientists skeptical of such treatments, which are time-consuming and expensive. However, in a promising study reported in 2014, 104 children with ADHD randomly received either neurofeedback or cognitive training (CT) in school. Compared to the kids who received CT, those who received the neurofeedback training had faster and greater improvement in their ADHD symptoms. Six months later, these improvements were still apparent.[3]

Retraining the Ear

Another approach targets listening skills. The Tomatis Method is a technique that was developed by a French ear, nose, and throat specialist, Dr. Alfred A. Tomatis. It uses music at different frequencies to retrain the way people with ADHD listen to and hear sounds.[4] Scientific studies on children with learning disabilities and behavior problems have shown that the Tomatis Method can help them to improve their social and academic skills and increase their attention span. A detailed analysis of five studies, published in 1999 in the *International Journal of Hearing*, found that this method can also be helpful for people with ADHD. They have difficulty sifting through all the stimuli in their environment. (Stimuli can be anything that demands attention—a conversation, a running dog, hot water, the sound of glass hitting the floor.) In the Tomatis Method, people with

ADHD can learn how to concentrate on certain sounds while tuning out background noise.

Additional Drug-Free Treatments

Some other alternative treatments include:

Cranial electrotherapy stimulation (CES): In this type of therapy, electrodes are attached to a patient's earlobes. A small handheld device powered by batteries administers low doses of electrical current to the skin and scalp muscles.

LENS: Developed by Dr. Len Ochs in 1992, LENS claims to enhance the brain's ability to adapt to a task, using weak electromagnetic fields to stimulate brain wave activity in areas of the patient's brain where connections are sluggish. Before treatment, the patient's brain is "mapped" to show areas of high or low connection. Areas of low connection appear like an aerial photograph of a blacked-out city.

Working memory training: Working memory is the ability to hold on to information long enough to accomplish a specific goal. Individuals with ADHD often have difficulty with this task. Working memory training uses computer game formats to exercise the working memory. ADHD patients can use these programs on a home computer. CogMed, a company that develops these "brain games" claims that they help reduce symptoms of inattention and hyperactivity in kids with ADHD. They point to scientific studies that back up their claims.[5] However, most medical experts do not recommend memory training as a viable treatment option for children with ADHD.

Interactive metronome (IM): Developed in the early 1990s, IM uses a computerized version of the metronome, an instrument that makes a regular ticking sound to help train musicians keep to the beat. The patient synchronizes

Future Directions in Research and Treatment

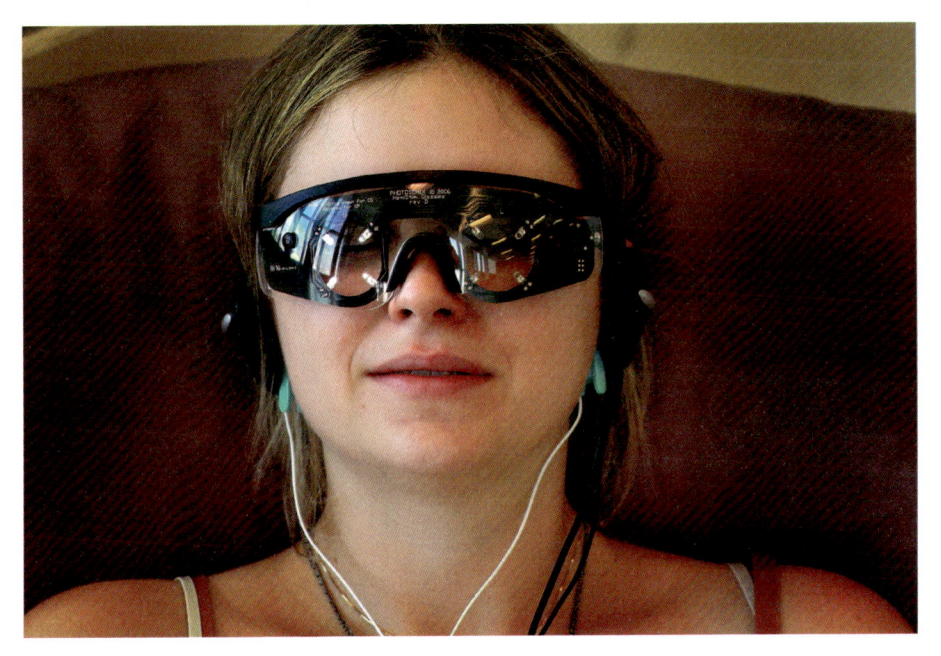

A woman wears therapy goggles and a cranial electrotherapy stimulator. CES delivers low doses of electrical current to the muscles of the skin and scalp.

hand and foot exercises to a range of precise tones heard through a headset. One study showed that IM therapy benefited a group of boys with ADHD for a wide range of activities. It may help patients to maintain focus longer as well as improve language and reading skills.[6]

DEVELOP HEALTHY HABITS

What you eat can have an effect on how well your brain works. Even though ADHD is not caused by eating too many sugary foods, a healthy diet provides the body with important nutrients that help to keep your brain connections strong. In fact, studies have shown that kids do better at school when they eat a nutritious breakfast. Eating a substantial amount of protein at breakfast is especially helpful. It supplies building materials for the formation of new brain connections and is also a longer-lasting source of energy than carbohydrates (sugars).

You may have heard that fish is good "brain food." That's because it contains omega-3 fatty acids, which belong to a healthy group of fats. Salmon, tuna, and sardines contain large amounts of omega-3 and are very important in a person's diet. Studies have shown that kids who don't get enough omega-3 fatty acids in their diet are much more likely to be hyperactive, have learning disabilities, and have behavior difficulties. In addition, eating too many foods loaded with saturated fats (the unhealthy fats) may actually interfere with the body's ability to use the omega-3 fatty acids. (Foods such as potato chips, cheeseburgers, pizza, and frosted cupcakes are all high in saturated fats.) Doctors now recommend that children with ADHD supplement their diets with more omega-3 fatty acids.

Exercise is good not only for the body, but for the mind as well. Researchers have found that physical activity increases the levels of the two important neurotransmitters—dopamine and norepinephrine—that help people calm down and focus. Many people with ADHD find exercise helpful in managing their

THE POWER OF SELF-DISCIPLINE

In 2004, an eighteen-year-old named Michael Phelps swam his way to eight medals, six of them gold, at the summer Olympics in Athens. Four years later in the 2008 Olympics, Michael took home eight gold medals. Michael now holds the all-time record for most Olympic gold medals (eighteen), and his twenty-two medals make him the most decorated Olympic athlete of all time.

Michael had always loved swimming, and excelled when he was in the water, but in the classroom he just couldn't concentrate. Michael was diagnosed with ADHD when he was nine and started on Ritalin. The diagnosis was a blow to the family: "It just hit my heart," says his mother, Debbie. "It made me want to prove everyone wrong. I knew that, if I collaborated with Michael, he could achieve anything he set his mind to."

Debbie, who had taught middle school, teamed up with Michael's instructors to get him the extra attention he needed in class. When she noticed he was having trouble paying attention in his math class, she hired a tutor and suggested that he design word problems that matched Michael's interests, such as "How long would it take to swim 500 meters if you swim three meters per second?"

In sixth grade Michael told Debbie he wanted to stop taking his Ritalin. Even though it made him less jumpy, Michael felt he was using the drug as a crutch. He felt embarrassed in school when the nurse would remind him to take his medication in front of his classmates. He wanted to try to control his behavior using only his own mental strength. With a doctor's help, he weaned himself off the drug. Over time, the focus and self-discipline Michael acquired in his swim training carried over into his schoolwork and other aspects of his life. In an interview he said, "Your mind is the strongest medicine you can have. You can overcome anything if you think you can and you want to."[7]

What You Can Do About ADHD

NATURAL BENEFITS

Could a stroll through the woods be good for your mental health? Possibly. In a national study, spending time in nature—"green time"—helped to reduce ADHD symptoms in children ages five to eighteen. In all, 452 children with ADHD were studied. During the study, the kids participated in activities that took place in three different settings: indoors; outdoors without much greenery, such as in parking lots; and outdoors in greener areas, such as parks, backyards, and tree-lined streets. Parents kept track of and recorded their children's behaviors after activities. Later, researchers concluded that children who spent time in nature were calmer and could concentrate better. They also had less trouble following directions and completing tasks. For example, playing outside in backyards or in open fields reduced ADHD symptoms much more than playing inside in the gym or playing basketball outside on paved surfaces. "Green time" may allow a reduction in a child's medication. It is also helpful for children who cannot take ADHD drugs.[8]

These children attend a camp for ADHD and similar disorders. Some research has shown that spending time outdoors has a positive effect on behavior and focus.

Future Directions in Research and Treatment

A young boy hugs a horse that is part of an equine therapy program. Working with the horse helped the boy, who has ADHD, learn patience and impulse control. Alternative therapies like these can have a beneficial effect when used as part of a complete ADHD treatment plan.

condition. Fifteen-year-old Kat Orlov, for example, used to spend four hours a day trying to finish her homework because of her disorder. Then she signed up for the crew team and started working out a couple of hours every day. She still takes ADHD medication, but exercise has helped a great deal: "When I exercise," she says, "I feel much more energized and awake. I have more of a feeling to sit down and get something finished."[9] Now it takes her half the time to do her homework.

Exercise can also help ease depression and anxiety. When the body is active, chemicals called endorphins work in the brain to produce "happy" feelings. Exercise can also make people feel good about themselves, giving them a sense of accomplishment, strength, and independence.

• 93 •

Although many of these approaches have shown promising results, much more research still needs to be done. More sophisticated brain-imaging tools may eventually be able identify a biomarker for the condition and aid in diagnosis. Cutting-edge genetic techniques may provide a better understanding of the processes underlying the disorder. In the meantime, many kids and adults have found success in a combination of drug treatments and behavior therapy. For these people, finally having some control over their lives has made a world of difference.

Top 10 Questions and Answers

Is there a cure for ADHD?
ADHD is a chronic condition, which means that an individual diagnosed with the disorder may experience various ADHD symptoms for life. However, these symptoms may change as he or she grows into adulthood.

My brother was just diagnosed with ADHD. I heard that it runs in the family. Does that mean that I have it, too?
Your brother inherited genes for ADHD, which means it is possible—but not certain—that you have it, too. Siblings have a 30 percent chance of sharing the disorder, and identical twins have an 82 percent chance. You should also be evaluated by a mental health professional.

Can eating too much candy give me ADHD?
Eating too many sweets does not cause ADHD. The sugar in candy could give you a burst of energy for a while, but after it wears off, you're back to your old self. ADHD is a condition that you have all the time, whether you eat sweets or not.

I'm confused. Is it ADD or ADHD? I hear people use both terms. Which is it?
ADHD is a general term that includes three types of attention disorders. One of them is ADD. ADD includes symptoms of inattention, but not hyperactivity.

There's a kid in my class who is always getting into trouble. Could he have ADHD?
Possibly, but there are a lot of reasons why a kid could be acting up in class. He could be reacting to a tough family life, or he may feel insecure and need attention. Teachers, counselors, and mental health professionals can work together to make a proper diagnosis.

My parents think that my sister might have ADHD. Is that possible? Only boys get that, right?
No. Boys are three times more likely than girls to be diagnosed with ADHD. That's because many of them have hyperactive symptoms, which are easy to notice. Girls are equally likely to qualify for the diagnosis of ADHD, but they tend to remain undiagnosed. Some girls may have the inattentive type of ADHD, or ADD. They may go unnoticed because they typically sit quietly and daydream.

Can kids grow out of ADHD?
Some children do grow out of it. Hyperactivity, in particular, tends to decrease as a child gets older. However, two-thirds of kids with ADHD will still experience symptoms of the disorder when they become adults.

Is ADHD a *real* problem, or is it just an excuse to misbehave? According to the American Psychiatric Association, ADHD is an official medical condition. There is a problem in the way the brain works. Treatment can help people with ADHD control their behavior better.

Growing up, I always felt like I was stupid. I had such a hard time learning things in class compared to everyone else. Recently, at age twenty-two, I was diagnosed with ADHD. Does that mean I'm not stupid after all?
People with ADHD are not stupid. In fact, most of them have average or above average intelligence. There are many people with ADHD who are doctors, lawyers, teachers, artists, writers, inventors, and pro sports players.

Are there any good things about ADHD?
There is no question that having this disorder profoundly affects people's lives, but not only in negative ways. For instance, *Psychology Today* reported in 2009 that individuals diagnosed with the disorder are 300 percent more likely to start their own business than individuals without ADHD. Positive traits often associated with ADHD are high energy, creativity, persistence, and a willingness to take on challenges.

Timeline of ADHD

495 BCE—The Greek physician Hippocrates describes ADHD-like symptoms.

1798—Sir Alexander Crichton, a Scottish-born physician and author, writes "An Inquiry into the Nature and Origin of Mental Derangement," in which he describes a condition he terms "mental restlessness" and which sufferers often call "the fidgets."

1845—German doctor Heinrich Hoffmann publishes "The Story of Fidgety Philip," the first accurate description of a child with ADHD.

1902—English pediatrician George Still documents a number of cases involving impulsiveness. He believes the cause is medical rather than psychological.

1917–1918—An encephalitis outbreak leaves patients with ADHD-like symptoms. Doctors later use the term *brain damaged* to describe all hyperactive children.

1937—Dr. Charles Bradley discovers that stimulants work to calm down hyperactive children.

1955—The Food and Drug Administration (FDA) approves Ritalin to treat psychological disorders.

1960—New York child psychiatrist Stella Chess coins the term *Hyperactive Child Syndrome*. She believes that hyperactivity is not caused by brain damage, but that something is abnormal in the brain.

1967—Ritalin is prescribed specifically to treat children with ADHD.

1968—The APA releases the second edition of the *Diagnostic and Statistical Manual of Mental Disorders (DSMII)*, which includes "hyperkinetic impulse disorder" for the first time.

1970—*The Washington Post* publishes a story stating that 5–10 percent of schoolchildren in Omaha, Nebraska, are being given stimulants like Ritalin to control their behavior. The article generates a storm of controversy about the medication of children and the prevalence of ADHD diagnoses.

1970s—ADHD is identified in adults.

1973—Dr. Benjamin F. Feingold claims that hyperactivity is caused by an overload of sugar and food additives in the diet.

The Rehabilitation Act of 1973 adds an additional qualification for schoolchildren with ADHD.

1980—The American Psychiatric Association officially names the condition *attention deficit disorder*, or *ADD*.

1990—Dr. Alan Zametkin, and a team of National Institute of Mental Health (NIMH) researchers, discover that brain activity is different in people with ADD than in those without ADD.

1994—The American Psychiatric Association renames the disorder *attention-deficit/hyperactivity disorder (ADHD)* to include behaviors with or without hyperactivity.

1996—The World Health Organization (WHO) warns overuse of Ritalin has reached dangerous proportions.

1999—Results from the largest study of ADHD treatment to date, known as the Multimodal Treatment Study of Children with Attention-Deficit/Hyperactivity Disorder (MTA Study), is published in the *American Journal of Psychiatry*.

2000—Fourth edition of *DSM* is published, listing three subtypes of ADHD.

2001—The International Consensus Statement on ADHD, containing the signatures of more than eighty of the

Timeline of ADHD

world's ADHD experts, reports that ADHD is a medical condition and can be treated with medication just like other mental disorders.

2003—The FDA approves Strattera, the first nonstimlant treatment for ADHD.

2006—The FDA approves the first skin patch (Daytrana) to treat ADHD in children ages six to twelve.

2007—The FDA approves a new stimulant drug for ADHD, Vyvanase, which is less likely to be abused than other amphetamine-type stimulants.

2009—A second nonstimulant drug, Intuniv (guanfacine), is approved by the FDA for treatment of ADHD.

2010—The FDA approves Kapvay (clonidine), a third type of nonstimulant drug, for ADHD.

Chapter Notes

Chapter 1. Life in Overdrive

1. David Lennon, "Film Chronicles Andres Torres' Battle with ADHD," *Newsday*, June 2, 2012, http://www.newsday.com/sports/columnists/david-lennon/film-chronicles-andres-torres-battle-with-adhd-1.3757904.
2. Centers for Disease Control and Prevention, "Attention-Deficit/Hyperactivity Disorder (ADHD): Data and Statistics," *CDC.gov*, December 10, 2014, http://www.cdc.gov/ncbddd/adhd/data.html.
3. National Institute of Mental Health, "Attention Deficit Hyperactivity Disorder (ADHD)," accessed March 14, 2015, http://www.nimh.nih.gov/health/topics/attention-deficit-hyperactivity-disorder-adhd/index.shtml.
4. Anxiety and Depression Association of America, "Adult ADHD," accessed March 14, 2015, http://www.adaa.org/understanding-anxiety/related-illnesses/other-related-conditions/adult-adhd.

Chapter 2. ADHD Throughout History

1. "ADHD Timeline," *Stuff4educators.com*, accessed March 14, 2015, http://stuff4educators.com/index.php?p=1_111_AD-HD-Timeline.
2. Ibid.
3. National Institute of Mental Health, "Attention Deficit Hyperactivity Disorder (ADHD)," accessed March 14, 2015, http://www.nimh.nih.gov/publicat/adhd.cfm.
4. Russell A. Barkley, *Attention-Deficit Hyperactivity Disorder: A Handbook for Diagnosis and Treatment, Second Edition* (New York: Guilford Press, 1998), 3–4.
5. Edward M. Hallowell and John J. Ratey, *Driven to Distraction* (New York: Pantheon Books, 1994), 270–271.

Chapter Notes

6. Stella Chess, "Diagnosis and Treatment of the Hyperactive Child," *New York State Journal of Medicine* 60 (1960): 2379.
7. Ibid., 2379–2381.
8. International Food Information Council Foundation, "Taking the Hype Out of Hyperactivity," *KidSource Online*, last modified July 25, 2000, http://www.kidsource.com/kidsource/content3/ific/ific.hyper.foods.k12.3.html.
9. National Institute of Mental Health.
10. National Institute of Mental Health, "The Multimodal Treatment of Attention Deficit Hyperactivity Disorder Study (MTA): Questions and Answers," revised November 2009, http://www.nimh.nih.gov/funding/clinical-trials-for-researchers/practical/mta/the-multimodal-treatment-of-attention-deficit-hyperactivity-disorder-study-mta-questions-and-answers.shtml; David Rabiner, "New Results from the MTA Study—Do Treatment Effects Persist?" June 2004, http://www.helpforadd.com/2004/june.htm.

Chapter 3. Understanding ADHD

1. Dav Pilkey, "The Almost Completely True Adventures of Dav Pilkey," *Dav Pilkey's Extra Crunchy WebSite O'Fun*, accessed April 21, 2015, http://www.pilkey.com/pdf/dav-pilkey-bio.pdf.
2. Deirdre Donahue, "'Captain Underpants' Jockeys for Attention," *USA Today*, August 20, 2003, http://www.usatoday.com/life/books/reviews/2003-08-20-captain-underpants_x.htm.
3. John M. Grohol, Psy.D. "Problems & Diagnoses Related to Childhood ADHD," *PsychCentral.com*, accessed March 12, 2015, http://psychcentral.com/lib/problems-diagnoses-related-to-childhood-adhd/00017152.
4. Linda Bren, "ADHD: Not Just for Kids Anymore," *FDA Consumer*, November–December 2004, 15.
5. Wendy Thurm, "Is There an ADHD Epidemic in Major League Baseball?" *SB Nation,* June 29, 2012, http://www

.sbnation.com/2012/6/29/3104332/is-there-an-adhd-epidemic-in-major-league-baseball.
6. Kimberly Holland and Elsbeth Riley, "ADHD by the Numbers: Facts, Statistics, and You," September 4, 2014, http://www.healthline.com/health/adhd/facts-statistics-infographic#6.

Chapter 4. Diagnosing and Treating ADHD

1. Molly Zametkin, "Growing Up with ADD—A Personal Perspective," *The ADHD Report*, August 2006, 14–16.
2. Ibid.
3. Ibid.
4. Maggie Koerth-Baker, "The Not-So-Hidden Cause Behind the ADHD Epidemic," *New York Times Magazine*, October 15, 2013, http://www.nytimes.com/2013/10/20/magazine/the-not-so-hidden-cause-behind-the-adhd-epidemic.html?pagewanted=2&_r=1&.
5. Michael I. Reiff, *ADHD: What Every Parent Needs to Know*, 2nd ed. (Elk Grove Village, Ill.: American Academy of Pediatrics, 2011), 73.
6. Alan Schwarz, "Thousands of Toddlers Are Medicated for ADHD, Report Finds, Raising Worries," May 16, 2014, *New York Times*, http://www.nytimes.com/2014/05/17/us/among-experts-scrutiny-of-attention-disorder-diagnoses-in-2-and-3-year-olds.html.
7. Tiffany Lankes, "ADHD Putting Strain on Schools," *Herald-Tribune,* June 27, 2004, http://www.heraldtribune.com/apps/pbcs.dll/article?AID=/20040627/NEWS/60127007; Tiffany Lankes, "Schools Close to Settling Mom's ADHD Suit," *Herald-Tribune*, October 28, 2005, http://www.heraldtribune.com/apps/pbcs.dll/article?AID=/20051028/NEWS/510280489.

Chapter 5. Living Well With ADHD

1. Joseph Biederman, "Turning Adult ADHD Around," July 12, 2005, *Play Attention: Attention Deficit*, http://www

Chapter Notes

.playattention.com/attention-deficit/articles/turning-adult-adhd-around/.
2. Ibid.

Chapter 6. Future Directions in Research and Treatment

1. The University of Sydney, "New Breakthrough in Diagnosis of ADHD," February 18, 2010, http://sydney.edu.au/news/84.html?newsstoryid=4501.
2. Madlen Davies, "Doctors Could Soon Diagnose ADHD in Children with a Brain Scan," *Daily Mail*, September 15, 2014, http://www.dailymail.co.uk/health/article-2756747/Doctors-soon-diagnose-ADHD-children-brain-scan.html.
3. Arlene Karidis, "Therapists are using neurofeedback to treat ADHD, PTSD and other conditions," January 19, 2015, http://www.washingtonpost.com/national/health-science/therapists-are-using-neurofeedback-to-treat-adhd-ptsd-and-other-conditions/2015/01/16/b38e6cee-5ec3-11e4-91f7-5d89b5e8c251_story.html; Jon Hamilton, "Train the Brain: Using Neurofeedback to Treat ADHD," *NPR*, November 1, 2010, http://www.npr.org/templates/story/story.php?storyId=130896102; N. J. Steiner et al., "In-school Neurofeedback Training for ADHD," *Pediatrics* 133, no. 3 (March 2014): 483-492, http://www.ncbi.nlm.zed+Control+Trial.+Journal+of+Pediatrics.
4. Pierre Sollier, "Finding Solutions That Offer Hope and Confidence," *ADD & ADHD*, © 2001–2006, http://www.tomatis.com/English/Articles/add_adhd.html; Pierre Sollier, "Research," The Tomatis Method, © 2001–2006, http://www.tomatis.com/English/ Articles/research.html; Tim Gilmor, "The Efficacy of the Tomatis Method for Children with Learning and Communication Disorders," *International Journal of Listening* 13 (1999): 12.
5. ADDitude editors, "Four Brain Training Therapies for ADHD Children and Adults," accessed March 15, 2015, http://www.additudemag.com/adhd/article/6563-4.html.
6. Ibid.

7. Judy Dutton, "Parenting Advice from Michael Phelps' Mom," accessed March 15, 2015, http://www.additudemag.com/adhd/article/1998.html; Marilyn Wedge, Ph.D., "From ADHD Kid to Olympic Gold Medalist," September 4, 2012, https://www.psychologytoday.com/blog/suffer-the-children/201209/adhd-kid-olympic-gold-medalist.
8. Frances E. Kuo and Andrea Faber Taylor, "A Potential Natural Treatment for Attention-Deficit/Hyperactivity Disorder: Evidence From a National Study," *American Journal of Public Health* 94, no. 9 (September 2004) 1580–1586.
9. Liz Szabo, "ADHD Treatment Is Getting a Workout," *USA Today.com*, March 26, 2006, http://www.usatoday.com/news/health/2006-03-26-adhd-treatment_x.htm.

Glossary

amphetamine—A type of stimulant drug that is sometimes abused to get a "high" (feelings of intense happiness and increased energy). The amphetamines used for ADHD are not addictive when taken in the prescribed doses.

antidepressants—Drugs used to treat depression.

anxiety disorder—A condition that causes stress and panic.

attention deficit disorder (ADD)—A condition characterized by an inability to concentrate, pay attention, and/or control one's actions.

attention-deficit/hyperactivity disorder (ADHD)—A term used to describe attention disorders with or without hyperactivity.

behavior modification—A treatment often used to change unacceptable behavior in people with ADHD.

cerebellum—A region at the lower back of the brain. It helps to control and coordinate movements and is also involved in attention and the processing of language and music.

cerebral cortex—The outermost layer of the brain. We use it to think, remember, make decisions, and control the movements of the body.

coexisting conditions—Two or more health conditions that are present in the same person. Individuals diagnosed with ADHD often have a coexisting condition, such as dyslexia or depression.

combined type—A type of ADHD in which a person shows both inattentive and hyperactive-impulsive symptoms.

depression—A condition that causes severe sadness and hopelessness.

distractible—Having an attention that is easily turned to something else.

dopamine—A neurotransmitter chemical that works in the brain to help control behavior.

frontal lobe—The part of the brain that helps a person concentrate, make plans, and think before acting.

gene—Hereditary material inside body cells that carries information about a person's characteristics.

hyperactive—Restless, unable to concentrate for any length of time, having a need for continual physical activity.

hyperactive-impulsive type—A kind of ADHD combining both hyperactivity (restlessness, inability to concentrate) and impulsivity (acting before thinking).

hyperfocus—A symptom of ADHD in children and adults who concentrate intently on one thing for an extended period of time.

IEP (Individualized Education Program)—A written education plan designed to meet a child's learning needs.

impulsivity—Acting before thinking.

inattentive type—A kind of ADHD in which the person has difficulty paying attention.

inherited—Passed on by genes from parents to children.

learning disability—A condition that makes certain areas of learning difficult, such as reading, written expression, or mathematics.

neurofeedback—A technique that monitors brain-wave patterns and rewards changes in behavior, leading to a desirable result.

neurotransmitter—A chemical that carries messages from one part of the brain to another.

norepinephrine—A neurotransmitter chemical that works in the brain to block distractions and focus attention.

PCBs (polychlorinated biphenyls)—Industrial chemicals commonly found in water and air pollution.

positron-emission tomography (PET) scan—A test in which a radioactive substance is injected into a patient and then tracked as it travels through the arteries of the body.

Glossary

receptor—A protein on the surface of a cell that picks up particular kinds of neurotransmitters, hormones, or other chemicals.

Ritalin—A stimulant drug (methylphenidate) used to treat ADHD.

self-esteem—How you feel about yourself.

stimulant—A drug that makes a body system more active, making most people feel more alert and energetic.

stimuli—Things in the environment that attract attention or produce mental or physical reactions.

Strattera—A nonstimulant drug (atomoxetine) used to treat ADHD.

toxin—A poison.

working memory—The ability to remember and use relevant material while in the middle of an activity.

FOR MORE INFORMATION

Attention Deficit Disorder Association (ADDA)
add.org
> ADDA provides information, resources, and networking opportunities to help adults with ADHA lead better lives.

Centers for Disease Control and Prevention
cdc.gov/ncbddd/adhd
> Founded in 1946, the CDC is the nation's health protection agency. This site provides research, articles, statistics, and tools for coping with ADHD.

Children and Adults with Attention-deficit/Hyperactivity Disorder (CHADD)
chadd.org and *help4adhd.org* (National Resource Center on ADHD)
> This national nonprofit agency works to improve the lives of affected people through education, advocacy, and support.

Learning Disabilities Association of America
lddaamerica.org
> LDAA supports and promotes the success of individuals with learning disabilities across all aspects of life.

National Institute of Mental Health (NIMH)
nimh.nih.gov
> The largest scientific organization in the world is dedicated to understanding and treating mental illnesses.

For More Information

Camps & Schools Serving People With ADHD and Special Needs

adhd.kids.tripod.com/camp.html

This list includes:

Landmark College in Putney, Vermont

Pima Academy in Tucson, Arizona

Stone Mountain School at Camp Elliott in Black Mountain, North Carolina

Vail Valley Learning Camp in Vail, Colorado

Further Reading

Brinkerhoff, Shirley. *Attention Deficit/Hyperactivity Disorder*. Broomall, Pa.: Mason Crest, 2015.

Chesner, Jonathan. *ADHD in HD: Brains Gone Wild*. Minneapolis: Free Spirit Publishing, 2012.

Denevi, Timothy. *Hyper: A Personal History of ADHD*. New York: Simon & Schuster, 2013.

Goodwin, Tracey Bromley, and Holly Oberacker. *Navigating ADHD: Your Guide to the Flip Side of ADHD*. Bloomington, Ind.: AuthorHouse, 2011.

Kershner, Tad. *Living with ADHD*. Edina, Minn.: ABDO, 2011.

Spodak, Ruth, and Kenneth Stefano. *Take Control of ADHD: The Ultimate Guide for Teens with ADHD*. Waco, Tex.: Prufrock Press, 2011.

INDEX

A
Adderall, 42, 52, 64
ADHD
　causes, early research, 23–28
　genetic role in, 48
　misdiagnosis, overdiagnosis, 56, 64
　name changes, 21
　overview, 6–7
　types, 37–43
alcohol, 48–50, 72–74
alpha waves, 85
amphetamines, 20, 23, 27, 42, 52, 59–65
anxiety, 49, 62, 93
attention deficit disorder (ADD), 10, 21, 25–26, 43

B
baseball, 42
Beethoven, Ludwig van, 33
behavioral issues, 13, 16–18, 35–37, 44, 49
behavior evaluation form, 57–59
behavior modification, 13, 27, 51–52, 65–66
Bell, Alexander Graham, 33
Benzedrine, 20
beta waves, 85
biomarkers, 81, 94
blood doping, 42
boredom, 36
Bradley, Charles, 20
Bradshaw, Terry, 33
brain, 26, 45–48
brain scans, 81–82
brain wave patterns, 85
buproprion, 64

C
Captain Underpants, 29, 31
Carrey, Jim, 33
causes, 43–50
cerebral cortex, 45
Cher, 33
Chess, Stella, 23
clonidine, 64
CogMed, 88
cognitive training, 87
combined ADHD, 43
coping mechanisms, 55, 74–80
counseling, 66–68
cranial electrotherapy stimulation, 88

Crichton, Alexander, 14–16

D
Daytrana (skin patch), 65
delta waves, 85
depression, 49, 64, 72, 93
Derry, Joanie, 68–70
Dexedrine, 52
diagnosis, 25–26, 55–60, 74, 81
diet, nutrition, 25, 43–45, 90
Disney, Walt, 33
distracted driving, 75
DNA, 47
dopamine, 46–48, 61

E
Edison, Thomas, 33
Einstein, Albert, 33
Eisenhower, Dwight D., 33
endorphins, 93
exercise, 7, 55, 68, 76, 90–93

F
Feingold, Benjamin, 23–25
fetal alcohol syndrome (FAS), 48–50
Franklin, Benjamin, 33
friends, relationships, 13, 35–38, 43, 49, 66–68, 80
frontal lobe, 26, 46, 82

G
gender differences, 44
Gigante, 9
Granata, Cammi, 33
guanfacine, 64

H
Hippocrates, 14
history, 14–20
Hoffman, Dustin, 33
Hoffmann, Heinrich, 16–17
homework, 38, 43, 46, 52, 55, 78, 93
Hyperactive Child Syndrome, 23
hyperactive-impulsive ADHD, 40
hyperactivity, 10, 37
hyperfocus, 12

· 111 ·

I
inattentive ADHD, 40–43
Individualized Education Program (IEP), 70
Individuals with Disabilities Act (IDEA), 70
IntegNeuro, 81
interactive metronome, 88–90

J
Jergen, Robert, 72–76
journaling, 74–76

L
lead paint, 50
learning disabilities, 35, 43, 49, 68–71
LENS, 88

M
Mandel, Howie, 33
Mozart, Wolfgang, 33
MRI, 55, 74
Multimodal Treatment Study of Children with ADHD (MTA), 26–28

N
National Institute of Mental Health (NIMH), 25–27
nature, green time, 92
nerve cells, 46
neurofeedback, 82–87
neurotransmitters, 46–48
norepinephrine, 46–48, 64

O
Ochs, Len, 88
omega-3 fatty acids, 90
Orlov, Kat, 93

P
PCBs, 50
performance-enhancing drugs, 42
Phelps, Michael, 91
physical exam, 57
Picasso, Pablo, 33
Pilkey, Dav, 29–31
positron-emission tomography (PET), 25–26, 55
prevalence, 10

R
Rehabilitation Act of 1973 Section 504, 70–71
risk factors, 37, 43–50

Ritalin, 23, 27, 42, 59–64, 91
Roof, Gene, 8

S
salicylates, 25
schizophrenia, 74
school accommodations, 68–71, 78–80, 91
SMR waves, 85
social skills, 27–28, 80
specialists, 57
Spielberg, Steven, 33
spinal tap, 20
steroids, 42
Still, George, 17, 19
stimulants, 20, 23, 27, 42, 52, 59–65
Strattera (atomoxetine), 64
sugary foods, 43–45
suicidal ideation, 64
support groups, 74, 76
symptoms, signs, 8–10, 29–31, 35–38, 44

T
theta waves, 85
toddlers, 64
Tomatis, Alfred A., 87
Tomatis Method, 87–88
Torres, Andres Yungo, 8–11
treatment
  alternative, 82–90
  antidepressants, 64
  behavior modification, 13, 27, 51–52, 65–66
  counseling, 66–68
  historically, 20
  listening skills, 87–88
  MTA study, 26–28
  nonstimulant drugs, 64
  side effects, 62, 64, 65
  stimulants, 20, 23, 27, 42, 52, 59–65
twins studies, 48

V
Visser, Susanna, 64
Vyvanase, 62

W
Williams, Robin, 33
working memory training, 88

Z
Zametkin, Alan, 25–26, 51
Zametkin, Molly, 51–55

5/19/16